STRIKER

CLOSE
RANGE

NICK HALE

STRIKER

CLOSE
RANGE

NICK HALE

EGMONT

Special thanks to Michael Ford

To James, for your creativity and enthusiasm

EGMONT
We bring stories to life

Striker: Close Range first published in Great Britain 2010
by Egmont UK Limited
239 Kensington High Street, London W8 6SA

Text copyright © Working Partners Ltd 2010

The moral rights of the author have been asserted

ISBN 978 1 4052 4964 5

1 3 5 7 9 10 8 6 4 2

A CIP catalogue record for this title is available
from the British Library

Typeset by Avon DataSet Ltd, Bidford on Avon, Warwickshire
Printed and bound in Great Britain by the CPI Group

One look at the guys waiting for them in passport control and Jake knew he and his dad were in for more trouble. The men blocking their way didn't look like normal airport staff – they were too well dressed: the cut of their suits designer, not airport issue. And what was with the mirrored shades? Jake couldn't see the guy's eyes as he handed over his passport, but he could feel himself being inspected closely. Then his passport was taken away, a phone call made.

Jake looked over to where his dad was getting the same treatment. His dad shrugged, as if to say it was no big deal. Beside him was the air stewardess, Bernedetta, who had personally escorted them off the plane and fast-tracked them to here. Jake tried to shake off his nervousness around the beautiful Italian woman as memories of the flight on Igor Popov's private jet came flooding back. The air stewardess on board had killed three people and nearly crashed their plane.

After five minutes, he and his dad were waved through, and Jake began to believe he might simply be paranoid. As they reached the stairs to the baggage reclaim area, Bernedetta wished them a pleasant stay in Milan. She handed Jake's dad a small piece of paper, and said in a low voice, 'Call me if you get bored.'

His dad smiled politely and pocketed the number. 'Doesn't hurt to keep the fans happy,' he said to Jake as they headed into the baggage hall.

While they waited for their bags, Jake took out the Brother-hood Tournament brochure, the reason they were coming to Milan. Well, the *public* reason. Jake was in no doubt that his dad was here for entirely different purposes. His dad had been very clear, though. After they were both nearly killed in Russia, he wanted Jake as far from danger as possible.

The four-nation tournament had been set up to raise money for humanitarian causes in Africa. Jake's dad had been called by the organisers to do English-language commentary on Sky for the games in which England appeared. The England vs Germany game was seen by many to be the showpiece. Following that would be England vs Spain. In the final match, at the end of the one-week event, England would take on the hosts, Italy.

And Jake would get to see it all – one of the best things

about having a dad who was not only a former footballer, but also a well-connected spy with the British government.

They wheeled their cases into Customs. Jake noticed his dad was limping again. The world thought the great Steve Bastin had a career-ending injury in Munich, 1988, which left him with a permanent limp. But that was all part of his MI6 cover. He must have been pretending so long it came as second nature. Jake found he was smiling. After sixteen years of secrecy, of only seeing his dad in the holidays from private school, he was finally getting to know the man who hobbled beside him. And more than that − for the first time, Steve Bastin was a father too.

The queue out through Customs was backed up as guards with German shepherds emptied out some guy's case. He complained in a language Jake didn't recognise, and the guard nodded to two of his colleagues, who stepped in at either side. The man tried to move away, but they grabbed him and forcibly led him off, the contents of his luggage still strewn across the table.

'I wonder what that's about,' Jake said.

'Security's tight everywhere these days,' his dad replied. 'Just take it easy. We've got nothing to hide.'

You've got plenty to hide, thought Jake. *Just not in your suitcase.*

They walked through into Arrivals. A sea of faces greeted them: an elderly couple looking on expectantly; a woman and her toddler daughter waiting, probably, for a husband and father; several chauffeurs holding up boards with names – Ursillo, Ettiami, Lima.

'Jake!'

And then a face he recognised. His mother. She was standing a row back from the front of the crowd, waving excitedly. Jake waved back. She crossed the rear of the crowd to where the arrivals spilled out on to the main concourse. Jake pushed his trolley along, then abandoned it as she threw her arms round him.

'I'm so pleased to see you!' she said, squeezing him tightly. 'You've grown! Again!'

Jake wasn't sure about that – they'd last seen each other in Paris three months ago. He did notice he was slightly taller than his mum, which hadn't been the case before. Jake's mother had been a model in the eighties and early nineties. He'd seen a few clippings of his mum and dad from the papers, but it wasn't like now when players and their partners got followed around night and day by paparazzi.

But football and modelling had something in common: after thirty, you were thought of as 'past it'. Luckily, both of Jake's parents were good at adapting. Where his dad had

4

been welcomed into coaching and commentating roles, his mum had jumped to the other side of the camera lens to be a fashion photographer.

Jake broke away as his dad walked up behind them. His mum's smile remained, but without the same spark.

'Steve,' she said.

'Hayley,' he said back. Jake thought his dad's body language was a bit stiff as he gave her two pecks on the cheeks. She kissed the air either side of his face. They may as well have shared a limp handshake, for all the warmth there.

Jake never knew the real reason for their divorce, but he remembered the arguments clearly enough: sitting in his bedroom, listening to, but not really understanding, the raised voices downstairs. Having experienced firsthand his dad's ability to lie, it must have contributed, he supposed.

'Good flights?' she asked. 'How was Russia?'

Jake shared a look with his father. If only she knew.

'Pretty tame,' Jake said. Apart from the plane crash, the murders, the bomb, the fights, his dad getting shot . . .

'Great,' she said. 'Good for you two to spend some time together.'

His dad shrugged. 'He didn't cramp my style *too* much.'

Jake raised his fists to send a playful jab at his dad, but his mum cut in.

'What's that on your head, Jake?'

Suddenly the mood was lost. Jake had forgotten about the scab on his forehead – a memento from his fight with the recently deceased footballer/criminal Devon Taylor. He pulled his fringe forwards.

'It's nothing, Mum.'

'Let me see,' she said, pulling him towards her. Jake didn't fight it – what was the point? His mother pushed back his hair. Jake saw her eyes widen.

'It looks worse than it is,' he said.

'It *looks* terrible!' she said. 'Are those stitches? How could you let this happen, Steve? That will scar!'

Jake felt sorry for his dad. 'It's not his fault, Mum. I was messing around . . . up a tree.'

His dad arched an eyebrow. Jake knew the excuse was lame, but it was the first one that came to mind. His dad would have to coach him on the fine art of fibbing. He could never tell his mum that the fight with Devon was one of the least life-threatening events in Russia.

His mum sighed. 'You're old enough to know better, Jake. And *you* . . .' she stabbed a finger towards his dad '. . . I trusted you to look after him.'

His father's face stiffened in anger. *Here it comes*, thought Jake – *the inevitable argument*.

6

But Jake's dad just shrugged. 'You're right, Hay. I was too busy . . .'

What's he doing? Jake wondered.

'You're *always* too busy!'

'So,' his dad continued. 'Maybe Jake should stay with you this week. Keep out of harm's way.'

Hold up! thought Jake. *Why does he want to get rid of me? He must be up to something for MI6.*

'I think that's a very good idea,' Hayley said.

'Don't I get a say in this?' Jake said. There was no way he was going to miss out – on the football *or* the mission.

'That's settled, then,' his dad said. He patted his jacket as a mobile phone rang. He pulled it out, looked at the display and frowned. 'I need to take this. Wait here, will you?'

Jake was silently fuming as he watched his dad stride off. *He's probably going to make some covert calls. He's already shrugging me off.*

'If he's going to make us wait,' his mum said, 'we might as well make use of the time.'

Jake gave up on staring angrily after his father. He turned back to his mum only to come eye to lens with her camera.

'That's it,' said Jake's mum, snapping away. 'Pout a bit more. Yeah, you look really moody.'

Jake held out his hand, feeling his cheeks flush. 'Mum, stop it! This is *so* embarrassing.'

His mum stepped to one side, and snapped Jake's profile. The camera looked like a traditional optical 35mm, but Jake knew it was a state-of-the-art digital. 'Stand straighter. Don't look at the camera. Look like you're pissed off.'

'I *am*,' Jake muttered, but he couldn't help smiling. People were starting to notice the impromptu photo session happening in their midst. They probably thought he was someone famous.

'Right, now sit on your bag,' his mum said. 'Lean over, elbows on knees, hands clasped between your legs, head up, turn left.'

Jake did what she asked.

Three clicks in quick succession. 'That's great, Jake.'

'It's hardly the most amazing spot in Milan,' he said as his mum stood up and readjusted the focus. 'An airport terminal.'

His mum walked over, reviewing the pictures. 'You'd be surprised. I've been doing so much studio work recently. My agent says there's a good market for the informal stuff.'

'I'm pretty sure no one wants pictures of me, though,' he said.

His mum peered closer at the little screen. 'What are you talking about? You're a good-looking young man. Especially with that rugged scar.' She pursed her lips. 'A pity it's real.'

'Mum, I said, it wasn't Dad's −'

'Seriously, though,' she interrupted. 'You could get into modelling, Jake. You've got good musculature, and you look at least nineteen −'

'That's enough!' he said. His dad was returning. Thank God. He didn't know which was worse: posing for more photos or the idea of strutting down a catwalk.

His mum had turned to snap the new arrivals, trying to capture the joyful moments when their eyes fell on waiting loved ones.

'What's up?' his dad asked. He looked a little anxious.

'Mum's working,' Jake said, gesturing to her.

He noticed two men talking to each other and looking over at them. *Great!* thought Jake, as the men started making a beeline towards them. *More autograph hunters.*

The men came through the crowd and Jake noticed they were some sort of officials. Both wore a uniform of navy trousers and light-blue shirts, with a badge on their chests. Not Customs, that was for sure. Their faces were impassive; now Jake came to think about it, they didn't look like fans. Finally, as they emerged through the crush of bodies, Jake spotted they had automatics holstered at their hips.

'*Mi scusi, signore,*' one said with a heavy Italian accent. 'Would you like to follow us?'

It wasn't a question.

Jake took half a step towards his dad, but the other man side-stepped and dropped his hand to his gun. 'This is not your business.'

Jake's dad took a small step backwards, and raised his hands in surrender. The posture looked friendly, but Jake knew from his boxing classes that you put your hands up so they were better positioned to block or counter punch. It was a self-defence trick.

'What's this about?' his dad asked.

'*Per favore*, Mr Bastin. We'd like to ask you some questions in private.'

The man who hadn't spoken was eyeing Jake like he was something he'd just scraped off his shoe. There was a challenge in his stare that said, *Just try it, kid.* Or whatever 'Just try it, kid' translated to in Italian.

Jake returned the look, without blinking.

His dad maintained his subtle defensive posture. 'Look, if you'll just tell me . . .'

The speaker stepped forwards and grabbed Jake's dad's upper arm firmly. Jake noticed his father stiffen. Jake half expected him to break the hand away and snap the idiot's arm, but he looked across at Hayley. Jake's mother hadn't noticed what was happening and was still clicking away.

'Fine,' his dad said. 'Jake, tell your mum I'll be back soon.'

The men led his dad away, holding an arm each.

Jake followed a few steps. 'Dad, what . . .'

His dad looked back over his shoulder. 'Jake, stay here. I'm sure it's just a misunderstanding.'

Jake stopped and watched his dad go. This wasn't right. Were the men police, or not? They hadn't shown any ID. Did Italy have Secret Police? What if they loaded him into a car outside? Drove him somewhere? Jake prickled with indecision. He knew he should do something.

But with his mum here, what could he do? The last thing Jake wanted was to blow his dad's cover.

'Get off me!'

Jake spun round at his mum's voice. He struggled to make sense of what he was seeing. Two figures, both dressed head to toe in black, wearing balaclavas, were attacking his mother!

2

'Hey!' shouted Jake. One of the attackers had one hand round his mum's waist, the other on the camera round her neck.

With a vicious yank, one of the masked men pulled the camera and its strap from Hayley's neck. Jake went at him first, diving into his legs with a rugby tackle. He scythed the attacker down, but the guy was quick. He freed his arm from Jake's grip and offloaded the camera to his accomplice, who caught it and started running.

The one beneath Jake backfisted the bridge of his nose, bringing a white explosion of pain. Jake fell back as the attacker wriggled free and went in the opposite direction.

Jake blinked the tears away and sprang up. His mother was pale with shock, but unharmed.

Jake sprinted along the terminal concourse. The attacker carrying his mum's camera was twenty metres ahead, but a crowd of Japanese tourists, all wheeling huge suitcases, chose that exact moment to pass ahead of him.

But instead of skidding to a halt the attacker took a light step up on to a case, and leapt high over two more carts. The tourists let out a collective gasp as the attacker sailed through the air and landed gracefully in a standing position.

What the . . .! thought Jake. *I'm dealing with some sort of ninja.*

The assailant with the camera turned and looked back for a moment, then set off again.

'Out of the way!' Jake yelled, waving his arms.

The tourists didn't move fast enough, and Jake tripped over a fallen case. He sprawled across the polished floor, but pulled himself up. Ahead, Jake saw the attacker heading towards automatic doors at the far end leading outside. There were two security guards standing off to one side, sipping espressos at a café bar.

'Stop him!' Jake shouted. They turned lazily. '*Attenzione!*' Jake tried, pointing. Slowly, they understood. One jogged across to block the fleeing thief, another unclipped his radio.

The thief saw and veered off sideways. He leapt over a set of seats, legs spread into the splits to clear the heads of dozing travellers, and headed towards an emergency exit. Jake cut across the diagonal to close the distance between them. When the man reached the door, he slammed down the handle and burst through. Jake was ten metres behind. *There's no way in hell you're getting away from me.*

They were outside, where green-and-white taxis lined up to take arrivals away to their destinations. As the attacker sprinted across the taxi lane, one blasted its horn, brakes screeching. Smoke climbed over the wheels. For a moment, Jake thought it would collide with the thief, but the fleeing man deftly sidestepped away, bracing with his hands against the bonnet. As he made to run again, Jake leapt and slid feet-first across the bonnet. He reached and his hand closed on the camera.

'Got you, you scum!' he said. He tugged at the camera, but the strap was wound round the thief's wrist.

At the doors, across the taxi rank, Jake saw the security guards emerging.

'Over here!' he shouted, clinging to the camera with all his strength.

He felt a sharp pain in his kidney, and went down on one knee. Then another blow to his neck. Jake cried out and fell against the bonnet, feeling the camera slip out of his loosened grip. The other attacker was standing over him. He stepped back to stamp on Jake's head, but Jake dodged and the foot caught the camera, smashing it into the metalwork of the car.

Jake rolled off the bonnet, and brought up his fists. His blood was pounding. He moved sideways to keep one attacker in front of the other, and sent a jab at the closest. The thief weaved. Jake followed up with a feint, then sent a blow into the guy's stomach. It connected with a satisfying thump. With a grunt, the thief doubled up. Jake was following with a knee to the face when the second attacker twisted and sent a roundhouse kick into his jaw. Jake had no chance. He spun round, lost his balance and managed to get a hand out before he hit the tarmac. His shoulder crunched into the ground, but he kept his head up. As he rolled over, he watched the black-clad assailants sprint off through a flowerbed. More car horns blasted.

The security guards arrived at his side as Jake steadied himself on an elbow. The camera, with the lens broken into several pieces, lay on the ground in front of the stalled taxi, whose driver was standing amazed behind his open door.

'Va bene?' said one of the guards. 'You OK?'

Jake stood up and brushed the grit off his clothes. His jaw felt like someone had hit him with a sledgehammer.

No, he thought, stooping to pick up the wrecked camera, *I'm not OK*.

Who the hell *were* those people?

*

Back in the terminal building, the security guards were speaking with his mum.

'I've told you,' she said. 'I don't know who they were.'

Jake held the pieces of camera in his open hands. 'I'm sorry, Mum. I couldn't stop them.'

Her face fell as she spotted the camera. 'Oh, it's ruined!' she cried. 'Are you all right, though?'

'I'll live,' he said.

His dad arrived at their side. 'Sorry I took so long.'

Jake tried to catch his dad's eye to see what was up, but his mum got in first. 'Never there when you're needed . . .' she sighed.

'What are you talking about?' his dad asked, stepping forwards and reaching for Jake's mum. 'Are you all right? What's happened?'

She batted his arms away. 'We were *attacked*,' she said.

Jake's dad looked at the security guards, then Jake.

'They were trying to steal Mum's camera,' Jake said.

'We have many pickpockets in the airport,' said the security guard. He motioned to the camera, or what was left of it. 'It is best not to have such expensive objects on display.'

His mum's face flushed. 'If you did your job better . . .'

While his mum started ranting, Jake pulled his dad aside. 'They weren't pickpockets, Dad.' He remembered how the attacker had vaulted over the luggage trolley, their clothes, the way they'd fought. 'They were professionals.'

His dad's tongue played inside his cheek as he thought. He looked over at Jake's mum, who was still arguing with the security guards.

'Dad, what's going on?' hissed Jake.

His dad shook his head. 'I don't know.'

Jake's temper flared once more. His dad was clearly holding something back.

'And what happened to you?' he said. 'Who were those people you went off with?' He added, sarcastically, 'People from Sky Sports?'

The security guards were taking some details down from his mum who stood with arms akimbo looking ready to blow her top again.

'Very funny,' whispered his father. 'They were immigration people – just had a couple of things to check with my papers.'

Jake could tell when it was no use pushing.

'Come on,' said his mum, walking over. 'I've had about enough of airports for today.'

His dad seemed only too happy to oblige, and muttered something to his mum about Italy having a bad reputation for pickpockets. Jake trailed after them, replaying the attack in his mind. Pickpockets didn't wear balaclavas. Nor were they typically trained in ju-jitsu, or whatever it was. This had something to do with his dad's mission, for sure, but it seemed to have taken everyone by surprise.

3

'Hi, this is Steve Bastin. I can't take your call at the moment, but . . .'

Jake hung up for the third time that morning. Why had his dad switched off his phone? He was probably doing some sort of covert work. But after all they'd been through in Russia he wouldn't let himself be shut out.

Equally, his dad might be in the studio, going through technical checks and preparing for his commentary duties on the Brotherhood Tournament. Either way, it didn't make Jake's day any less boring. His mum had woken him up at the crack of dawn saying she needed an assistant on her latest shoot.

Hayley was in the kitchen of her tiny Milan apartment – Jake could hear the Gaggia machine gurgling from the lounge. This flat was in the Zona Tortona, an up-and-coming area of high-end fashion boutiques and cafés. Most people in the street below looked like they belonged on the catwalk, and Jake guessed that appealed to someone like his mother.

Jake tried his dad again with the same result. He'd do anything to get out of this photo shoot. Standing around while his mum took pictures was *not* how he planned to spend his time in Milan.

Hayley walked into the sitting room, sipping her coffee. She'd tied her hair back, and was dressed simply in jeans and T-shirt, which looked plain but Jake knew had probably cost hundreds of euros. 'You ready?'

'Do I have to?' Jake asked, giving his best cheeky grin – the one he used to pull when he was eight and she didn't want to let him out to play football. 'I could just stay here and watch TV.'

'No way,' Jake's mum said. 'Your dad might be happy to leave you alone in strange cities, but I'm not. And I might need your muscles to shift a few things for me. There'll be models there . . .' She left it hanging.

Jake saw it was useless to resist. 'Well, if you *really* need me.'

'Thanks, Jake.' She ruffled his hair like he was a kid. He guessed he deserved that for the eight-year-old grin. 'Anyway,' she said, 'it would be good to spend more time together, wouldn't it?'

She also knew how to play the guilt trip.

'I guess so,' Jake said, peeling himself off the sofa.

'Good,' she said, then pointed to a bag near the coat stand. 'Since you're such a strong lad, you can carry my camera case.'

Last week he was dodging bullets in a rooftop restaurant. This week he was a carthorse. How things had changed.

His mum drove like a maniac, even by Italian standards. She threw the little Fiat 500 round corners as though she was in a rally, finding gaps in the traffic where Jake couldn't see one. For the most part, Milan could have been any other commercial European city, but Jake saw occasional signs to galleries and museums and other tourist attractions. He caught glimpses of the Duomo – the main cathedral – rising above the buildings around.

'You'll be learning to drive soon, I guess,' she said. 'You're seventeen next year.'

Jake gripped the door for support as she squeezed the car between a truck and a 4x4. If either had swerved, they'd have been crushed like a tin can.

'I might ask Dad to teach me,' he replied.

'What's that supposed to mean?' she asked, glancing at him with the hint of a smile.

They left the main road, and headed between tall office blocks.

'Will there be anything for me to do at this shoot?' Jake asked.

'You can help dress the models, if you want,' his mum said, winking.

'Mum!' Jake protested. He squirmed in discomfort.

'I'm just saying, no drooling, no trying to chat them up.' She was smiling a little. 'These girls are professionals.'

Were all mothers like this? 'I'm not going to hit on them.'

Soon the office blocks gave way to smaller shops, and the architecture became more traditionally Italian. Stucco buildings, washing hanging out across the street.

'Seriously, I need you to be on your best behaviour,' his mum said, as they stopped at a crossroads. 'This Granble shoot is a big deal.'

'Who's Granble?' asked Jake. 'Some up-his-own-arse designer?'

'Far from it,' his mum said, suddenly very businesslike. 'Anders Granble owns the Granble Diamond Company. He's South African. A very, very wealthy man.'

'I've never heard of him,' Jake said.

'That's not surprising,' his mum replied. 'It's quite a new company. He used to be in marketing at De Beers diamonds, but he's gone his own way. Found new mines on the border with Botswana. No one thought there were any diamonds there at all . . .'

'But they were wrong?' Jake asked. This, at least, sounded vaguely interesting.

'Wrong in a big way. Apparently, Granble's rocks are flawless, which is rare. It makes them extra-prized and much more valuable.'

'So this is about showing them off,' Jake said.

'The main photo shoot is tomorrow, at the church we're heading to now. Then there'll be a flashier show at the last football game of the tournament.'

'England–Italy. At the San Siro?' Jake asked.

His mum nodded. 'I don't know if Granble is a big football fan, but he's an astute businessman. He knows the money in football. There's going to be a catwalk set up at half-time. Models will wear designer clothes as well as Granble's diamonds. He hopes to get some of the players' partners involved too.'

'Oh, please!' said Jake. 'WAGs strutting their stuff? It sounds like a nightmare.'

'Watch it, mister,' said his mother, laughing. 'You're talking to an ex-WAG, right here.' She turned into a cobbled square with a fountain in the centre. One side was dominated by a beautiful old church. She pulled up outside.

The stone of the church façade was pale, with a hint of ancient redness, blushed like a peach. The gable was cracked, with a fissure running diagonally through the bell-tower.

'Why here?' Jake asked, getting out. 'There must be a thousand actual studios in Milan.'

His mum started unpacking things from the boot of the car.

'Mr Granble's team wants to base the campaign around the idea of worshipping the perfect diamond. It's hard to get permission to photograph in a normal church, but this one's not used.'

'It looks like it's about to fall down,' Jake said.

'This place has been here for two hundred years,' his mum said, passing Jake a tripod. 'It's survived two earthquakes. I think it'll take more than a photo shoot to finish it off.'

The side door to the church was already open, and a man in a boiler suit stood at the side smoking. When he saw Jake and his mum approach, his flicked the butt to the ground and crushed it with his heel.

'*Buongiorno*, Signorina Maguire.'

'*Ciao*, Hector,' replied his mum. 'The lighting up and running?'

'*Si*,' he replied.

Jake's mum him into the dark interior, where the air was

24

much cooler. The church smelled musty and abandoned, and a bird of some sort fluttered across the beamed roof. Rows of pews and small chapels were arranged on both sides. The only light came from the slightly grubby stained-glass windows at the far end and along both sides. Most had bars covering the lower half inside. Choir stalls backed a large altar, and beside that was an enclosed lectern reached by a short set of steps. A mezzanine level loomed over the rear of the church.

Several people milled around the altar end, and from the assorted wires Jake guessed they were technicians. His ears picked up the chatter of female voices from a room off at one side, and his eyes caught the flash of flesh through a crack in a door. That must be where the models were getting changed.

He glanced away quickly, feeling his face redden. He didn't want to look like a pervert.

'So what do you think?' his mum asked.

'Uh . . . it's creepy,' said Jake, his voice echoing. 'You sure you want to do the shoot here?'

His mum laughed. 'Just wait,' she said. 'Hector, can you give us some light?'

'*Sì*,' said the Italian.

He barked an instruction, and one by one the lights flicked on. Jake squinted for a second while his eyes adjusted.

Spotlights on the floor sent shafts of light into the roof space, picking out the spinning columns of dust. Rigged on scaffolds around the walls, lamps blazed.

His mum clapped her hands together. 'Good, huh?'

Jake nodded slowly. The interior still looked neglected, but goth and cool.

'It certainly is,' said a voice from behind them.

Jake turned and saw two men. One, the taller, wore an expensive suit, and had fair hair and a reddish complexion. His companion was dressed all in black, with what looked like military trousers and, despite the weather outside, a thick turtle-neck sweater. He was carrying a silver briefcase, which Jake noticed was cuffed to his wrist.

Jake's mum walked right up to the first man and they kissed cheeks.

'Mr Granble, what an . . . unexpected pleasure,' she said.

Granble looked past her at Jake, and smiled. 'Well, you know how it is, Ms Maguire. I wanted to make sure my advertising dollars are being put to good use.'

His mum laughed, but Jake thought she sounded nervous.

'Today's just about getting the lighting right and setting up a few shots with the girls,' his mum explained. 'You really didn't have to come.'

Granble patted Jake's mother on the arm. 'Hayley, you

26

know me. I'm putting a lot of faith into this campaign. Into *you*. Everything has to go to plan.' Jake could feel the threat that lingered beneath the words, and bristled. Granble added with a smile, 'And I wanted to make sure Jaap here doesn't lose my diamonds.'

So *that* was what was in the case.

Again, his mother laughed nervously. Jaap, Jake noticed, didn't crack a smile.

'And who's this young man?' Granble asked, gesturing to Jake. His eyes travelled up and down his frame as though wondering what to make of him. There was nothing friendly in the look.

Hayley beckoned Jake to come over. 'Mr Granble, this is my son, Jake. He's staying with me for a few days. I brought him along to help out.'

Jake walked forwards and held out his hand. Granble tipped his chin, and looked down his nose. He didn't offer his hand in return. 'As long as he doesn't get in the way . . .'

His mum's brow creased a little, but she managed to keep the cheer in her voice.

'Right then, I best get on,' she said.

Jake held Granble's stare until the South African looked away. He wasn't going to let anyone push his mother around, even if he owned all the diamonds in South Africa.

Over the next half-hour more people arrived: two make-up artists, a florist, a hair-stylist and several assistants. Jake tried helping position things for the shoot, but with his shoddy Italian it was hard work. He felt he was just getting in the way. In the end, he settled for shifting unwanted pews to the back of the church.

The stylists all went through to where the models were sorting themselves out. Jake wondered what priests would think of the world's hottest women getting changed in their little dressing room.

Granble had brought staff with him too, two women in sharp suits with faces like hatchets. It soon became clear that their role was to act as the liaisons between their boss and whomever he wanted to bother. Mostly Jake's mum, it seemed. Jake had never seen her so anxious about work before. He realised for the first time what a big deal this was for her.

'Mum,' he said, after she'd spoken to Hector about moving some of the lights near the altar, 'can I help with anything?'

She twirled a loose ringlet of hair round her finger, and looked at something over his head. Jake saw out of the corner of his eye one of Granble's pit bulls heading their way.

'Sure, Jake,' she said, biting her bottom lip nervously.

She bent down and reached into her camera bag, and took out the battered camera that had been damaged in the airport attack. 'Could you have a look at this for me? I've got three days' worth of pictures on here that I can't afford to lose. It didn't work when I tried it at home, but you're better with technology than I am.'

Granble's raven-haired assistant arrived at their side ready with another question. *Better to get out of the way for a while.*

'No problem,' he said. 'I'll take a look.'

'How can I help you, Marissa?' he heard his mum say, her cheerfulness clearly fake.

Jake retreated to one of the side chapels. It was dominated by a stone tomb containing the bones of some saint or other. Ragged prayer cushions were stacked in one corner, so Jake took a couple and sat on the floor. He switched on the camera. The cracked screen lit up.

He scrolled through the pictures, but for some reason they weren't resolving properly on screen. Patches came up from each picture, but not the whole thing. One showed just the left side of Jake's body in the airport, but other parts were concealed in a haze of pixels. Was the problem with the digital file itself, or just the camera's display? The only way to find out would be to get the pictures on to a laptop and check them out. But Jake's computer was at his mum's apartment.

Outside, he heard his mother directing someone – a model. 'That's right – on one knee . . . Close your eyes . . .'

Jake wondered what his dad was doing at the stadium. If that's where he was. His mission in Milan might not even have anything to do with the Brotherhood Tournament. But why else would MI6 send an *ex-footballer* on the mission? It was the perfect cover. It had fooled Christian Truman in St Petersburg, and Igor Popov.

A bolt of excitement sparked through Jake's frustration. Had Popov resurfaced in Milan? Perhaps he was fixing matches, or something worse? No . . . Jake guessed Popov would be lying low for a while. He'd been cocky when they last saw him in Russia, but he wasn't stupid.

I'm wasting my time here! There's something big going on, and I'm sitting in an abandoned church fiddling with a broken camera.

Maybe this mission was something completely different. Terrorists? The Brotherhood tournament would be the perfect place to stage an attack, with the world watching. He wondered how tight security was at the San Siro.

Or an assassination! Italy's sports minister, Ignacio Lauda, had been a lawyer before, and brought down several Mafia families. Now he was tipped to be the next prime minister.

What if there was a hit man on his tail? Jake's dad would need help, another pair of eyes . . .

Jake forced himself to focus on the task at hand – skimming the photos, just to check they were all suffering from the same problem. It was as though water had been spilled across a traditional negative, blurring the pictures. As he continued to scan backwards, he found older images. Judging by the date-stamp, they were taken earlier in the day when Hayley had picked them up from the airport, and showed people in some candid Italian street scenes.

Jake paused when he recognised a face.

Abri . . .

Holy shit. Abri Kuertzen was the hottest model on the planet. South African, still under twenty, her face had already graced the covers of *Vogue*, *Elle* and *Cosmopolitan*. Not the kind of magazines Jake bought, but even *he* knew who she was. In fact, she'd presented an award for MTV a couple of months before.

'Found a quiet corner,' said a female voice.

Jake looked up, and did a double take at the face that looked down at him. Blue eyes, blonde hair cut short above perfect cheekbones. Lips that . . .

'Cat got your tongue?' said Abri Kuertzen.

4

Jake stood up quickly as Abri glided into the chapel. A supermodel – *the* supermodel – in the flesh. She was tall, only a few centimetres shorter than him, but her feet were bare. In heels she'd be taller. She was wearing a flowing white dress that came to her knees. Nothing special, but she looked, frankly, awesome.

'I'm Jake,' he said. 'My mum's the photographer.'

Duh! Make yourself sound like a kid, why don't you!

'I'm Abri,' she said, holding out her hand. 'I'm a professional coat-hanger.'

She said it with a straight face, and it took Jake a second to realise she was joking. He laughed, and her face split into a wide grin. Jake shook hands, hoping his palm wasn't clammy, and that he wasn't laughing at her joke too hard.

'I know who you are,' he said. 'I recognise your face . . . I mean . . .'

Don't sound like a stalker. Don't sound like a stalker.

'I get it,' said Abri, still grinning. Jake realised that he'd never seen that expression on her face before – in all the posters she was pouting, looking half asleep.

'So,' she said. 'You haven't answered my question. What are you doing in here?'

Jake shrugged, trying not to blush and thinking he'd got it about right. 'I think Mum wanted me out of the way.'

Abri pointed at the camera. 'Are you a photographer too?'

'Oh, no, I'm just trying to fix it for her. I'm a . . .' *Don't say you're at school!* 'I'm in Italy helping my dad out. He's a footballer. Steve Bastin.'

Abri's blank face suggested she had absolutely no idea who Steve Bastin was.

Typical! thought Jake. *The one time I actually want someone to have heard of my dad!*

'Do you play football?'

'Sure,' Jake said. 'Though not professionally. Yet.' Suddenly he felt stupid, and added by way of excuse, 'I'm only sixteen.'

Nice one, Jake. You may as well have said you're still in nappies!

'Hm,' said Abri. 'You look older. Bigger, y'know. I'm only seventeen.'

She bit her bottom lip. Was Abri Kuertzen checking him

out? Jake knew he was blushing now. An image flashed in his mind of Abri's latest campaign for Calvin Klein underwear.

Stop it, Jake!

'So, you having any luck fixing it?' she asked.

She reached over and placed her hand over the camera, bringing herself within centimetres of Jake. Her fingers slid under his and lifted the camera to look closer. His stomach lurched.

Was she flirting with him?

'I . . . I need to get it plugged into a computer,' he said. 'It doesn't look good. You can hardly tell what most of the pictures even show.' He released the camera, but stayed close to her.

'That's a shame. You seem to know your stuff.'

Jake was about to say that wasn't really the case, when one of the Granble reps, that raven-haired thirty-something with too much make-up and a too-tight skirt Marissa, poked her head round the wall. She pursed her lips when she saw Jake.

'There you are, Abri! Come now, please. We've got a reporter from *Avvenire* here to speak with you.'

'I'm coming,' Abri said, finally backing away. She smiled at Jake. 'Nice to meet you, Jake. Perhaps we'll catch up later, yes?'

'Yeah. Sure,' Jake said.

She held out the camera and Jake reached to take it. But it slipped from her hand too soon and fell to the floor.

'Oh!' she exclaimed.

Jake didn't have time to catch it, and stuck out his foot, cushioning the camera and balancing it on his shoe. With a deft flick, he launched it into the air and caught it.

'Show-off!' said Abri, winking. 'Perhaps you *should* go pro.'

After she'd gone, Jake waited for his heart to stop thudding.

Perhaps spy stuff could wait.

Jake went out into the main part of the church, carrying the camera. His mum was busy with two models by the lectern. One was a statuesque black girl with hair shorter than Jake's, the other a tanned blonde Jake thought he'd seen in a music video. She was standing on the lectern, resting her hands on an open Bible. Hands wearing glittering diamond rings, Jake realised. The other model stood beneath, wearing a dazzling necklace against her dark skin. Granble's female assistant looked on like a hawk, while Granble himself was sitting talking to Jaap in one of the pews. He clicked his fingers for his assistant to scurry over, and whispered something in her ear, which she then relayed to Hayley.

Jake saw his mum make adjustments in light of Granble's comments, but he could tell from her forced smile and stiff body language that she wasn't particularly happy with the interference.

He looked around for Abri, and saw her sitting in a pew near the back next to a glamorous-looking female reporter holding a Dictaphone. Jake didn't want his mum to think he was loitering, so he headed round the side of the church until he reached the doorway near the front, which opened on to the spiral stone steps. Abri noticed him and waved. Jake gave a wave back then headed up the narrow stairwell. It led to the mezzanine level above, which was covered in a thick layer of dust and scattered bird droppings. The boards creaked a little as Jake crossed them. He wondered for a moment if they were safe, then saw other footprints in the dirt, and figured he wasn't the first person up here. Presumably the lighting guys had checked it out as well.

He reached the edge, which was shielded with a balustrade, and peered over. At the far end of the church, his mother was still arranging the models. But it was the voices below that caught his attention. By some curious acoustics, Jake could hear the supermodel and the reporter talking very clearly below.

'And how have you enjoyed your stay in Italy so far?'

'Well, Lenka,' Abri said, 'you know that Italy is very close to my heart, because my mother is Italian . . .'

'So, Abri, how do you feel about wearing such beautiful diamonds?'

'You know what they say about a girl's best friend!'

It sounded like a pretty dull interview, and Jake was about to leave when the journalist asked a more interesting question. 'But you must have some reservations, as a South African, about wearing these specific stones. There have been so many protests. After all, the source of the diamonds is . . .'

'That's enough!' another woman's voice cut in.

Jake looked down and saw that Granble's black-haired rep, Marissa, had seized the reporter's Dictaphone.

'You can't do that!' the journalist protested.

'Wrong,' said Marissa. 'Please leave. The terms of the interview were clearly stated in the contractual agreement.'

With a few huffs and sighs, the reporter gathered her things and left the church, closely trailed by Marissa and Jaap. Jake thought it was time to leave too, and made his way back across the mezzanine. He noticed that the stairs continued upwards to the bell tower. A rope hung across, and part of the wall above had crumbled on to the stones. As he came back down the stairs, Abri was standing up from her pew.

'Hey, footballer,' she said. 'You following me around?'

Jake blushed. 'No, I . . .'

'I'm *kidding*,' she said. 'I wouldn't mind if you were.'

'Oh,' was all Jake could think to say.

'Listen, I've got a couple more shots to get done, but why don't we catch up later?'

Was a supermodel asking him on a date?

'Sure,' said Jake, trying to sound cool. 'Are you OK, though? I couldn't help hearing the end of the interview.'

'Oh, that,' she said. 'It was nothing.'

'It sounded like something.'

She laughed. '*You* sound like a detective!' Abri leant closer. Her breath tickled his ear. 'Some people don't like the way Granble operates his business, that's all.'

'Yeah,' said Jake. 'Granble and his people are, well, not what I'd describe as nice.'

Abri frowned, looked around, then lowered her voice.

'Between you and me,' she said, 'I think Granble is raping the continent, destroying the landscape and robbing the community of what is naturally theirs. He'll trample anyone to get what he wants.'

Jake was speechless. There was a new hardness in Abri's eyes that he hadn't seen before. 'So . . . why are you doing this campaign?' he asked.

Abri lowered her eyes. 'I do what my agent tells me,' she

said. 'I can't afford to get a reputation for being difficult at this stage in my career.' She looked at him again. 'You think I'm a hypocrite, don't you?'

Jake didn't know what to say, but he knew he couldn't voice what he was thinking – that if she wasn't hypocritical, who was?

'No, of course not,' he said. 'I just . . .'

He was spared an explanation when another model sauntered up the aisle. She was the blonde, and probably the second best-looking woman Jake had ever seen.

'Hey, Sienna,' Abri said, suddenly smiley again.

'The fitter wants you, Abs,' she said with a West Coast American accent.

Jake said, 'Hi,' but Sienna ignored him, took Abri by the arm and pulled her away. 'See you around, footballer,' Abri called.

'Oh, please!' hissed Sienna.

Jake watched them go into the vestry, and tried not to imagine Abri changing into her next outfit. It wasn't easy. His mum interrupted his reverie. She looked really stressed.

'Look, Jake, things are going pear-shaped here. We've got the wrong filters for the lights, one of the dresses is missing its train . . .'

Jake put his hands on her shoulders. 'Chill out, Mum,' he said. 'What can I do to help?'

His mum sighed. 'It's not that. I'm going to have to be away for a couple of hours sorting things out. Can you keep yourself busy? I'm really sorry . . .'

'Mum, that's fine,' Jake said.

His mum smiled and gave him a big kiss on the forehead. Jake looked around anxiously to make sure none of the models had seen.

'Great,' his mum said. 'How's the camera, by the way?'

Jake held up the broken camera. 'I'm not sure. I need to plug it into my laptop. Don't get your hopes up.'

But his mum was already looking to the front of the church, where Hector was up a stepladder.

'Not that one, Hector!' she shouted. 'Number three!'

Jake watched his mum walk briskly away.

A few hours of freedom.

And a dilemma: stay here with Abri, or use the time to find out what his father was *really* up to in Milan?

Hot girls or adventure?

The models were all in the vestry now, with the door closed. Who knew how long they'd be? And, though Jake had got on well with Abri – really well, in fact – Sienna didn't seem to be very friendly. Plus, if he knew anything about girls, it was that they took a long time to get ready.

Decision made, then. Girls would have to wait.

5

Jake traced the streets back the way his mother had driven. He guessed his dad would have to visit the Milan TV studios sometime that day to prepare for his official duties that night, commentating on England–Germany.

And if he's not there I'll track him down.

Jake looked for a taxi, but this area wasn't like the centre of the city. It was all small local shops – butcher's, baker's, hairdresser's – and most of the people he saw in the street were middle-aged or older. What he *did* spot was a bike shop with an emerald-green racing bike outside. Not the colour he would have chosen, but the gears looked good. He was checking the tyres when a short, stocky man in braces emerged. He was wearing a flat cap, but took it off in way of greeting, revealing a bald head.

'*Buongiorno*,' he said.

'*Buongiorno*,' Jake replied, using the bit of Italian he had picked up at school. He didn't want to *buy* a bike – just to borrow one for a few hours. What was the Italian for 'rent'?

They went back and forth for a while, with Jake trying to say he'd pay thirty euro for three hours. He mimicked riding the bike up the street and back again, but the shop owner seemed to think he meant he wanted a test ride.

Jake took out three ten-euro notes and showed his watch face, indicating the dial travelling round three times. Then the man understood, but he pointed to the watch as well. Jake shrugged. Surely he didn't want that, too? But the man went inside, and came out with a dictionary. He said the word 'deposit'.

So Jake handed over his watch, and the money, and climbed on to the bike. The owner came out with a battered orange helmet, and Jake put it on gratefully. If the Italians drove anything like his mum, he might need it.

He set off slowly, getting used to the bike. Soon he was pedalling steadily, and took a main road towards the city centre. The traffic became dense, but Jake was able to weave through on the bike. Taxis were the worst, cutting in front of him, and honking loudly when he returned the favour.

Jake's dad had said the main studio was on Edoardo Jenner to the north of the city, but he had to sneak a look at a tourist's map to find his way. He found Viale Edoardo Jenner, and cycled along it. It was a busy road, lined with offices and apartment blocks. He was beginning to lose hope of ever finding the place and thought about asking for directions, but then he saw it.

Milano TV.

The massive glass-fronted office block had a wide courtyard out front, and a fountain catching the sunlight in its spray. Potted fir trees lined the entrance. Jake hopped the bike up on to the pavement, swerved around a couple of suited men and skidded to a halt beside the front door. He didn't want to leave the bike outside in case it got stolen. So he wheeled it inside.

An enormous modern sculpture shaped something like a bull rested in the centre of the reception, surrounded by low-backed leather chairs and tables piled with TV and industry magazines. Against the far side, huge screens showed several TV channels silently.

Jake arrived at the desk, and the receptionist looked up.

'Hi,' said Jake.

'You have a delivery?' she said in English. 'Who for?'

Jake looked down at the bike. 'Oh, no, I'm not a courier. I came to find Steve Bastin. He's my father.'

The receptionist sighed loudly and checked her computer screen.

'Steve Bastin . . .' she said. 'He works here?'

'No,' said Jake. 'He's commentating, tonight.'

The receptionist clicked away on her keyboard. 'No, I have no one of that name.'

Jake calmed his frustrations. *He had to be here.*

'Maybe I should just go and look for him,' Jake said, pointing to the elevators.

'Not possible,' said the receptionist, losing her patience. 'All visitors must have passes.'

Jake could see he wasn't going to get anywhere, and was about to take his bike back outside when the elevator doors opened.

A small man, flanked by two security guards, stood within. Jake recognised him immediately as the Italian sports minister.

The security detail scanned the lobby for a moment, then strode across the reception area and ushered the minister out through the door. As they passed him, Jake caught a reflection of himself in the mirrored sunglasses of one of the guards.

I obviously don't look like much of a threat.

He pushed his bike outside and watched the sports minister climb into a silver limousine with tinted windows. One guard went in the back too, the other took the passenger seat. The car quickly pulled away.

Half a second later, two other cars moved as well — one, a BMW on the same side of the road; the other a Lexus across the street. The BMW followed in the limousine's wake, and the Lexus steered across a lane of traffic and slipped in behind the BMW.

It was too slick to be a coincidence. Sweat prickled on Jake's skin.

He hopped on to the saddle of the bike, and pedalled after the convoy. If something big was going to go down, he wanted to be there. His dad could thank him later.

They took the road behind Garibaldi Station, past small designer boutiques. The BMW was trailing fifty metres behind the limo, with the Lexus following one car after that. The traffic was fairly heavy, so it wasn't hard to keep up. Jake kept a few bike-lengths back from the Lexus, but he could see through the rear windscreen that there were two guys in the car.

They reached some lights, and Jake came up alongside, shooting a look into the front seats. One of the men, a mean-looking skinhead, was wearing some kind of communications earpiece and microphone. Was he linked in to the BMW?

When the lights switched, the minister's car took a left on to a tree-lined avenue. Jake saw they were approaching a major junction. Ahead of that was a large set of gates in ornamental gardens. Jake saw the word *cimitero* — cemetery.

Monuments and a chapel rose up behind iron railings. The cars he was following steered out into traffic, and Jake went after them, narrowly avoiding a pick-up truck whose driver eyed him with boredom through his open window.

This road was a major artery and the limo picked up speed. If the driver had spotted the tails, he wasn't taking any evasive action.

Lucky he's got me looking out for him, Jake thought, switching through the gears. He pumped the pedals to keep up, but the convoy was pulling away.

Jake saw a set of lights up ahead. As the minister's car went through, the lights switched to amber. The BMW accelerated through as it changed to red, and the Lexus jumped the light. These guys meant trouble. The other lane started to move and Jake skidded to a halt, slamming the handlebars with his fist. He was going to lose them.

As cars streamed across in front of him, he watched his targets recede into the distance. There was no way he could take the bike through that sort of traffic. He scanned the road up ahead, curving round the edge of the cemetery, and made a split-second decision.

Pulling the bike round, he hopped on to the kerb, and plunged through a side gate into the graveyard. A flock of pigeons burst from the path as he careered through them,

46

then dodged around two women pushing prams. Jake took the bike on to the grass, and hurtled across landscaped gardens. It was disrespectful, but he figured if there was going to be some sort of Mafia hit, then surely God could overlook it.

If the cars didn't go the way he hoped – sticking to the main road – he'd lose them. Treading the pedals, his legs aching, he whizzed down a narrow pathway between old crumbling headstones. The grass needed a trim here and it was tough going. Suddenly he saw a pile of earth ahead, and jinked the steering to avoid it. He saw a black space yawning.

An open grave!

With nowhere to steer, Jake yanked up the handlebars and lifted the front wheel as the two-metre abyss gaped below. As the wheel landed, he pressed down, dragging the rear of the bike with him.

That could've been nasty!

Twenty metres away a warden of some sort wearing a peaked cap shouted at him to stop, but Jake ignored him.

He almost missed the exit signs, skidding round to where another gate left the park. The road was just visible through thick bushes on the other side.

He slowed and switched through the gears to slalom through a set of railings. Out on the street again, he scanned up and down for the three cars.

The sweat cooled on Jake's head, but his heart was still pounding. He'd been in the cemetery for less than thirty seconds. If his mental map was right, this is where the cars should be.

But they weren't.

They must have turned off. *Damn it!*

Then he saw the limo. It was stuck behind a small red Fiat in the middle lane.

The BMW and the Lexus fell into its wake.

The minister's silver limo was indicating left. Jake dropped back on to the road, cutting across three lanes of traffic and jumped up on to the pavement on the other side, just as the limo turned into the road ahead of him. The buildings on either side blurred past, and Jake dodged carefully around the pedestrians on the narrow pavement, keeping level with the limo.

The driver had both the front windows down and looked nonchalantly to his right. His gaze lingered on Jake for a second, then he brought his eyes back to the road in front.

It's not me you should be worried about, Jake thought, *it's the hit men following you.*

He twisted to check they were still following. Yep. They were right behind.

The speed limit was 30kph, but Jake had to pedal hard

to keep up. The offices gave way to stone buildings as they entered the older section of Milan. With Jake's focus on the three cars, he was only vaguely aware of one of the greatest cities in the world flashing by him in a blur. Grand-façaded churches, massive palazzos, fountains in piazzas.

They reached a main square, behind which a cathedral's gothic towers soared into the sky. Tourists milled around everywhere in brightly coloured, mismatched clothes. *What was it about going on holiday that made people abandon their fashion sense?* As the cars went round the outside, Jake took a short cut up a ramp and found himself cycling behind a colonnade, between tables with coffee-drinking holiday-makers and café fronts. A waiter stepped out in front of Jake and gave a yelp, spinning away. Jake heard the crash of broken glass and shouted an apology over his shoulder. 'Sorry, um . . .' *What was it in Italian? 'Mi dispiace!'*

He reached some steps and juddered down. No suspension forks on a racing bike. When he saw the cars approach again, Jake realised that the Lexus had dropped off.

Huh? Perhaps it got caught in traffic.

Or maybe it had gone ahead to intercept.

Adrenalin surged through his blood, and he forgot about the burn in his legs.

Only one car was following now. And closer too, just one

car back. Jake slipped into the traffic again behind them, and thought he'd caught a glimpse of the driver looking in his rear-view mirror. He'd been careful, but they had probably recognised him from earlier. The bright green bike and orange helmet didn't help.

Well, there was nothing for it now.

The network of streets became more confusing, and quieter. The buildings on either side looked like they'd been put up in a hurry, and there were a few vacant lots filled with piles of concrete rubble and jutting steel rods. Cars were parked haphazardly beside the cracked pavements. Houses on either side looked empty, boarded up or shuttered for the siesta.

I guess the tourists don't come here, Jake thought. The minister's limo and the BMW were the only cars moving, apart from a dustbin lorry grinding up the street. If there was going to be a hit, this would be the place. Jake's blood ran cold. He hadn't really thought about what he'd do if things got heavy, but now he found himself wondering if he should call the police. Riding with one hand on the bars, thirty metres back from the cruising BMW, he reached into his pocket and took out his phone. Four missed calls from his mum.

He was still deliberating when the minister's limo indicated left and turned into what looked like a narrow road between tall apartment blocks. A couple of seconds later the pursuer turned as well. Jake free-wheeled after them, suddenly realising he didn't even know the emergency number in Milan.

It was gloomy on the road, and the brake-lights of the BMW glowed red. It stopped right up behind the stationary limo. No one got out. Jake jumped down from the saddle, resting the bike up against the wall beside a discarded mattress. He realised it was a dead end, blocked by a wire-mesh fence at the far end. Cautiously he stepped further into the alley. The engines of both cars had been killed.

Suddenly, with the excitement of the pursuit sapping away, this felt very real.

Too real.

6

There was an old-fashioned trash can at the side of the alley, and Jake took off the lid. Would it stop a bullet?

Both front doors on the BMW clicked open, and two guys unpeeled themselves from their seats. They certainly looked like hit men, both over six feet, built like rugby players on steroids. Jake took a step back, cursing himself for being so reckless.

Suddenly a screech of tyres made him spin round. A car had blocked the near end of the alley. The Lexus. The door popped and the driver emerged.

'*Chi siete?*'

Who are you?

He was trapped.

'I'm Jake. Jake Bastin. English. *Inglese. Capsice?*'

The men closed in on him from both sides. Jake gripped the metal lid, wondering if he could take one down and give himself time to get back out to the road. Stuff the bike.

The driver of the Lexus reached inside his black jacket.

He's got a gun.

Jake lunged at him, driving the dustbin lid into his chest. The man fell backwards heavily and Jake charged towards the Lexus blocking the alley entrance. He was about to leap over the bonnet when the door on the far side opened.

Oh, Christ . . . Another one.

Something hit him hard on the shoulder and it felt like his whole body was on fire. Pain shot along his limbs and seemed to grip him in a spasm. *What was happening?* The pain was everywhere, making it impossible for him to think or move. Jake rolled back across the bonnet and saw a man pointing something at him. A wire trailed loosely between his hand and Jake.

As Jake crumpled to the ground, a word floated into his consciousness.

Taser.

Jake's face hit the ground hard. He couldn't move a muscle. His hands were pulled roughly behind his back and cold metal handcuffs clasped his wrists.

He tried to speak, but his mouth wasn't working properly. He tasted blood, and felt as weak as a kitten. The man who zapped him hauled him upright and then flashed a badge.

A five-pointed star. Jake read the words *Repubblica Italiana*. And then heard another word – *Polizia*.

The police officer jabbered a few more words in Italian that Jake couldn't understand, but he didn't need to. *They think I was after the minister*, he realised. The policeman held open the car door, while another of the men pushed Jake inside, hand pressing his head down. He let his body fall into the seat, and closed his eyes.

Now he was in a world of trouble.

'Just call my dad,' Jake said for what felt like the hundredth time. He mimed a phone at his ear. *'Padre?'*

The young uniformed police officer leant with both elbows against the cell door, working a toothpick between his teeth. He smiled.

Does 'padre' *mean priest, or father?* Jake wondered.

'Steve Bastin,' he tried. He mimed taking a step back to kick a football. 'He's punditing the Brotherhood Tournament.'

The police officer eyed Jake for a couple more seconds, then stepped back from the door.

Slam!

With a sigh, Jake sat on the hard bench and leant back against the grubby wall. The holding cell was hardly built for comfort.

He'd tried to get them to call his dad as soon as they arrived at the station, but just like the guys in the Lexus, the desk sergeant wasn't interested. He looked at Jake as though he was a serious threat. He had a brief discussion with the guy who'd tasered Jake, and took his name. Several other officers came out to look at the suspected political assassin. Eventually, two big officers led him to a cell, removed the cuffs and shoved him inside. They'd confiscated his phone and wallet. Jake didn't even have any proper ID on him.

He tried to keep his despair down. He didn't even know in which police station he was being held. There must be dozens in a city the size of Milan.

Amid the wretchedness and anger, he was embarrassed. Of course the minister had a police escort.

Hit men? *Oh, please!*

As far as he could tell, he hadn't been formally charged with anything. But they must be thinking about it. Was it a crime to follow a politician through the streets? Assaulting a police officer, well, there could be no arguing with that. But how was he supposed to know they were *Polizia*? They hadn't identified themselves until after he took the first swing.

Jake ran his hands through his hair.

How could he have got it so wrong?

The cell door clicked open and two uniforms came in.

The same as before, and an older guy with white hair and a severe expression.

'Who do you work for?'

Thank God! thought Jake. *Someone who speaks English, at last.*

'I don't work for anyone,' said Jake. 'I'm in Milan with my dad.'

'You're lying to me.'

'I'm not,' said Jake. 'I'm only sixteen.'

The man's cheek twitched. 'Then why are you following Mr Lauda?'

'I didn't mean any harm,' said Jake. 'It was a mistake.'

'And this "father" of yours, he knows what you were doing?'

Jake finally felt he was getting somewhere.

'No,' he said. 'He's working as a pundit for the Brotherhood Tournament. His name's Steve Bastin.'

'The football player?' said the man, his eyes widening a fraction.

'That's right,' said Jake, smiling. *Dad's name has to come in useful sometimes.*

The man spoke to the officer accompanying him, and was handed a notebook and a pen. He held these out to Jake. 'Write his telephone number, please.'

56

Jake scribbled down the digits, and passed it back to the officer, saying, 'Thank you.'

It didn't hurt to be polite.

After what felt like an hour, Jake was ushered out along the corridor by a surly-looking officer with three-day stubble and sweat patches under his arms. He offered Jake a plastic cup of water, then opened a door to what looked like an interview room. The white-haired senior policeman was there, and beside him was Jake's father.

'Dad!' said Jake. 'Look, I'm really sorry, I . . .'

His father held up his hands, and spoke to the policeman in fluent Italian. He called him '*capitano*', so Jake guessed that was his rank.

The captain nodded and left the room, leaving Jake and his dad alone. In the silence that followed he could see the fury bubbling away under his father's features. He opened his mouth to speak, but his dad got there first.

'Jake, what the hell were you doing threatening a senior Italian politician?'

'I wasn't threatening him,' said Jake, feeling his temper flare. 'I was . . . I was just following him.'

His dad held his hands aloft in exasperation, then brought them down at his side.

'For God's sake! Why?'

Jake blushed. 'I thought he was being followed.'

'He *was*!' said his father. 'By a stupid sixteen-year-old boy.'

Jake knew his defence was weak. What good would it do to tell his father how sure he'd been that the minister was in danger? It would only make him look like an even bigger fool.

'Your mother has been frantic . . .' said his father. 'She says she phoned you, over and over, but you didn't pick up. She was in tears when she called me, and I had to leave in the middle of an interview with Mark Fortune. You know who that is? The England captain, Jake!'

'I'm sorry,' he said again. 'What else do you want me to say? It was a mistake.'

'You're telling me,' his dad said. 'You're lucky they've agreed not to press charges. I think it's only because they were embarrassed about having to restrain you with a taser.' His tone softened. 'Are you OK though?'

'I'm fine,' said Jake. He could feel a bruise where the charges had entered him, but nothing bad. Just wounded pride.

'Jake,' his father said, suddenly serious again. 'The game starts in a few hours. I can't let my employers down again. I'm on thin ice after this little escapade. I need you to be good and stay out of trouble.'

Despite his relief, Jake couldn't help feeling patronised. After all they'd been through in Russia, here was the 'great' Steve Bastin treating him like a kid all over again!

'Dad, I thought I was doing the right thing. I thought I was protecting the minister. That you, y'know . . .'

His dad nodded slowly, and gave a small smile. He looked around the room and checked the voice recorder wasn't on. 'You thought it was something to do with my job? Well, Jake, it isn't. And that's none of your business anyway. Got it? You could have been deported for this stunt, or worse. Let me look after my affairs. The right thing now is to stay with your mother, look after her . . .' he trailed off.

Look after her? thought Jake. *Weird way of putting it . . .*

'Come on, then,' said his father, standing up, and offering his hand. 'And let's keep this between us. The less Hayley knows the better.'

'Agreed,' Jake said, shaking on it.

They walked through the station without any hassle, and his dad spoke for a few moments with the captain, shaking his hand and repeating '*grazie*' several times in the conversation.

The young officer with the toothpick gave a sneer and sly wave as Jake climbed into his father's car outside. He felt like a teenager being picked up early from a party by his parents.

'I had to give him and his brother free tickets to the final,' said his dad. 'Plus a behind-the-scenes tour. Good to see the police's reputation for corruption is still valid.'

Jake gave a fake laugh, but his mind was no longer on the police.

I can keep a secret from Mum, he thought. *But if you think you can keep one from me, Dad, you're wrong.*

7

They drove back across the city towards the stadium.

'I did have a surprise planned for you tomorrow,' his dad said gravely, 'but I'm not sure you deserve it.'

Jake looked at his dad's face, and thought he saw the hint of a smile. 'Come on,' he said. 'I know I screwed up. There's no need to mess with my head.'

'Well, I thought you might like to do a bit of training while you're here. At the San Siro . . .'

'Oh my God, Dad, that's great!' said Jake. He'd only ever seen the stadium on the TV, the flares and the noise during the AC Milan–Inter Milan derbies. The Champions League final. It was one of the most iconic grounds in the world.

'Oh, and I forgot to mention,' said his dad, 'you'd be training with the England team.'

As the words sank in, Jake's mouth fell open. 'Are you serious, Dad?'

His father was beaming and gave Jake a glance. 'Sure I am. Mark Fortune said he'd show you a few tricks.'

Jake felt like sticking his head through the sunroof and whooping at the citizens of Milan, but perhaps that wasn't a great idea.

'I can't believe it!' he said. He hammered the dashboard with his palms. 'That's awesome!'

'Thought you might be pleased,' said his father, laughing. 'While we're on the subject of bribes, think of this as a pay-off to keep you out of trouble.'

As the city passed by, Jake was lost in his thoughts. He'd dreamed about playing with Fortune and the team: being called on in extra time and scoring the winning goal in the World Cup Final. Playing as a professional footballer was all Jake had ever wanted, and so far his parents had stood in the way. Sure, they let him play in school teams, and the occasional Sunday League match, but when it came to the big time they'd always put their parental feet down.

'It's too soon,' his mother would say. 'Concentrate on your school work.'

'Too soon?' Jake would reply. It'd be too late! Many players were signed by the time they reached their sixteenth birthday.

'It's not a long-term prospect,' was his dad's mantra.

Well, it had worked out all right for him!

Jake had always thought he knew the real reason they were so against it. Truth was, football had got in the way of his parents' marriage. The hours spent training, or away with the team, had gradually eaten into their time as a couple, driving them apart. With his dad changing teams, from Spurs to Liverpool, Jake's mum was forced to move with him, abandoning the life she'd built up. She needed to be near London for modelling assignments, so when his dad went up north it had been a real strain. Eventually the relationship had collapsed.

Well, that's what he'd believed until a fortnight ago. But perhaps the real reason was Steve Bastin's other activities. He'd have had to lie, and perhaps those lies had caught him out . . .

'You sure you aren't just trying to get me out of the way so you can bug some rooms?' said Jake, testing his dad's new-found sense of humour.

'I can tell Mark you're not interested, if you like?'

Jake guessed that was the signal to drop it.

The stadium rose up before them. The San Siro! Five columns ran along each side like giant springs, and the red girders that supported the stands jutted from the top. It looked more like a factory or power station than a football ground. The car park was mostly empty this time of day, but a few stewards in their fluorescent jackets milled around.

'I'm serious now,' his dad said. 'Let me take care of my own business. You concentrate on your football. Mark and I go way back, to when I was coaching the under-21s. Don't let me down.'

'I won't,' Jake promised.

As his dad reversed into a spot in the private car park on the south side of the ground, Jake noticed a black smudge on the front of his shirt.

'You gotta make yourself presentable, Dad,' he said, leaning forwards to brush it off.

His dad looked down. 'Oh, that. I must have forgotten to take it off in the hurry to save my firstborn from incarceration in a foreign prison — know what I mean?'

'What is it?' Jake asked, climbing out of the car.

'A transportable transmission device,' said his dad. Jake frowned. 'A roving microphone to you and me.'

They took a staff entrance into the ground, his dad flashing a security pass at the guard.

Inside, the ground looked pretty old-fashioned compared to somewhere like Wembley, or the Emirates. The carpets were worn down in the middle. Light fittings on ceiling tracks picked out grubby marks on the walls. As they signed in at reception, a runner with earphones and some kind of electronic clipboard came dashing up to his dad.

'Mr Bastin, you're needed in Comm Box Two right away.'

'Sure,' said Jake's dad.

They took a back route, through service corridors with linoleum floors, lined with insulated wiring. Then through a set of double doors marked 'AV Department'. There were lots of doors off one side of the central waiting area, with temporary signs pinned outside each. One read SKY SPORTS. Jake followed his dad through.

The room was bright, up-lit around the outside. One wall was all glass, looking out to the stadium, three tiers of stands rising steeply from the pitch, the giant digital clock. The stadium was filling up, and already the shouting had started. At least thirty players were scattered over the pitch, pinging balls between themselves.

In the room, a large mounted camera was facing towards an illuminated desk, and three steel chairs. Sitting on one was a man dressed in a slim-fit grey suit, with a runner checking the microphone on his shirt. His face was familiar but it took Jake a couple of seconds to realise who it was. His dad was taking his jacket from a hanger in an anteroom.

'Dad,' Jake whispered. 'Is that Frederico Alessi?'

His father straightened his tie in the mirror.

'Sure is,' said his dad. 'He'll be commentating along with me.'

Alessi was an Italian striker of the late seventies – way before Jake's time, but still a legend.

'Can you introduce me?'

His dad checked his cufflinks and then looked at his watch. 'Maybe later. I have to start soon.'

The make-up woman put her head round the door.

'Mr Bastin, I need you now, please.'

Jake followed his dad back into the other room. It was filling up now, with two people in shorts and T-shirts fussing over the camera. On the pitch below the players were finishing their warm-up. A guy Jake guessed was in charge was sipping from a polystyrene cup, and speaking into a mobile phone in Italian, while a runner brought a jug of iced water and laid it on the table.

Jake's dad took a seat, and the make-up lady brushed his cheeks with some kind of powder.

'You've forgotten the lipstick,' Jake joked.

His dad tried not to laugh.

Another suited presenter came in, nodding greetings to everyone, and took a seat beside Alessi. The director stepped up to him and whispered something in his ear.

The presenter frowned and leant across to Alessi and his dad. He spoke in English.

'It's not good, Mr Bastin. We're a runner down. Some sort of stomach bug.' He massaged his fingers over his temples. 'That means we can't get the team news from the coaches. We're screwed.'

Jake's dad looked at him. 'What if we send my boy?'

The presenter scoffed. 'We need a professional.'

'He knows the game as well as anyone,' said his dad. 'That OK with you, Jake?'

Jake grinned. 'Definitely.'

The director, who looked flustered, nodded. 'Paulo, link him up.'

A guy with a satchel came forwards and attached a microphone to Jake's neck and clipped on an earpiece. They went through a quick soundcheck, with all three presenters speaking through the intercom to Jake.

'You need to go down elevator four,' said the director in broken English, pinning a Sky Sports press badge on Jake's shirt. 'Go to the dressing rooms with Roberto.' He tapped the guy with the heavy-looking camera perched on his shoulder. 'There should be team people around. They'll be able to help you.'

They were hardly the most detailed instructions, but Jake

didn't care. He was going right into the belly of the stadium, where all the players would be nervously waiting. Roberto was quick for a guy carrying a cumbersome piece of equipment, and they weaved past all the assorted personnel from the other stations, took the elevator and were soon by the dressing rooms.

'Can you hear me?' said his dad.

'Got you,' Jake replied.

'Good. See if you can find Ebner. He's the man you need to speak to.'

If it was busy upstairs, down here it was organised chaos. There were physios, coaching staff, subs, security, players, match officials, all jostling around. Jake recognised dozens of faces, but hardly had time to put names to them. They pushed through to a holding area, where Jake spotted the England assistant coach, Karl Ebner, talking to a bunch of journalists. Jake joined the pack.

'We heard Smith was injured,' said one. 'Can you tell us about that?'

Ebner nodded. 'That's right. His ankle was still swollen from training, but he's had it on ice and he'll be on the bench.'

Jake relayed the information to the commentary box, and Alessi asked him about formation.

'Mr Ebner,' Jake shouted above the others. 'Will you be

going with a lone striker, or two up front?'

Ebner did a double take, presumably not used to seeing someone so young doing Jake's job. 'We'll see how it pans out,' he said. 'We'll probably keep things fairly tight for the first half, with Fortune dropping into a holding role, and the wingers tucking in.'

'But you've got Sanderson on the bench,' said Jake. 'Wouldn't he be better sweeping up? He played in that position for two seasons at Aston Villa. That would free up Fortune to move forwards. He's England's top goal-scorer, after all.'

Ebner looked gobsmacked. 'Yes, well . . . as I say, we'll see how things pan out.'

He excused himself soon after.

'Good work, Jake,' Alessi said.

Jake joined Roberto beside the dressing rooms to catch some footage of the players lining up. Jake noticed they were all wearing black armbands. On both teams. Had someone died? Was it an anniversary?

'What are they commemorating?' he asked the cameraman.

Roberto shrugged.

'You did well, Jake,' came his dad's voice over the earpiece. 'Why don't you find somewhere to enjoy the game? There's a pressbox down there somewhere.'

Jake watched the players stream out on to the pitch, with Fortune at the front.

One day, he thought, *that'll be me*.

He soon found out what the black armbands signified. As he was settling into a seat in the press area, watching the big screen, he heard the tannoy announcer: 'There will be a minute's silence to remember a gifted player who died recently – Devon Taylor.'

The players on the screen bowed their heads in remembrance and the press room was quiet too. Jake squirmed a little in his chair. Those paying respects knew nothing about the real Devon Taylor, the one who had tried to kill him in St Petersburg on behalf of his father, the one who'd been willing to let innocent people be blown to bits for a few million dollars.

As the whistle blew, Jake's negative thoughts drifted away and he became rapt with the game. Germany scored early when Jason Price, the England defender, sent a sloppy back-pass to the keeper, but Fortune took England to one-all just before half-time. The second half was slow at first, with both teams playing cagily, but Smith came on to big cheers in the sixtieth minute. His ankle seemed absolutely fine, and after five minutes he picked up a raking cross-field ball from Price, and drilled it into the bottom corner off the post. The defender had made up for his earlier blunder, and when the final whistle went, it was 2−1 to England.

Jake was still buzzing the next day as he and his mum drove to the stadium.

'And after the game, Dad introduced me to all the players,' Jake said.

'I'm not sure I like the idea of you mixing with all those older guys. I know what footballers are like.' His mum was all nerves again. She was going to check everything was prepared for the catwalk show that would take place at half-time during the big game between England and Italy at the close of the tournament.

'Mum!' Jake protested. 'Don't be so old-fashioned. They're not all like George Best these days. You can meet them after practice, if you want.'

He checked the clock on the dashboard: ten-thirty. Training was due to start at eleven. If it wasn't his mum driving, he might be worried about being late.

'I've had about as much football as I can take, thanks,' she said. 'Watching your dad get muddy for ten years was enough.' She turned into the stadium approach road. 'Anyway, I'll have plenty to concentrate on sorting out −'

Something hit the windscreen. His mum screamed and screeched the brakes, and Jake's stomach lurched. He saw pieces of shell and egg yolk drip down the glass.

'Oh my God!' his mum gasped.

Another egg splattered on the bonnet, and he heard shouts. At his door, he saw an angry face and a hand slammed on the window.

'What's the hell's going on?' he asked.

His mum flicked on the central locking. 'Granble warned me about this,' she said.

A crowd of people gathered around the car, wearing matching T-shirts with the slogan: *No to blood diamonds!* One carried a placard saying: *Granble hates South Africa.*

A woman stepped right in front of the car and pointed at them. She shouted something that Jake didn't understand and those around her took up the chant.

Jake was torn. He half wanted to get out of the car and fight them off, but they looked ready to turn nasty. Jake's mum beeped her horn in frustration, but a woman stepped forwards and kicked the car.

'Damn!' his mum exclaimed. 'Haven't they got anything better to do?'

'We need to get out of here,' Jake said, looking at all the furious faces.

72

'I know, Jake, but −'

There was a massive crash in the back of the car, and Jake instinctively bent over as splinters of glass showered over them. He twisted round to see that a jagged wooden block had been driven through the rear window, splintering glass on the seats.

'Mum! Are you OK?'

She was pale with shock, with glass in her hair, but she nodded.

'I think so.'

Uniformed guards and suited men stepped forwards and began pulling the protestors away. As soon as the path was clear, a guard waved them on. When they'd safely pulled up in a space, Jake noticed his mum was trembling.

'You're not OK,' he said.

She turned off the engine. 'I'm fine, Jake.'

'What was all that about? What's Granble done to wind people up so much?'

'It's complicated,' said his mum. 'When you're as successful as Granble, you make enemies.'

'But how did they know who you were?' he asked.

His mum sighed. 'Mr Granble said they were organised. Not just your standard demonstrators. These guys link up via chat rooms on the web. They've done some pretty bad things to protest back in South Africa. Criminal damage, arson. A model even got her face slashed, Mr Granble told me.'

Jake swallowed and looked at the broken window. A few hundred euros would sort it.

It could have been a lot worse.

Jake remembered what Abri had said back in the church, about Granble abusing his power.

'Mum, is there something dodgy about these diamonds? Y'know, like blood stones . . . conflict diamonds . . . you're *sure* Granble's mining these himself and not buying them off some warlord?'

'Everyone says he's legitimate,' his mum said. 'All his stones are certified.'

'Yeah, but documents can be forged. I saw this programme . . .'

'Listen, Jake,' said his mum. 'I'm not going to be lectured. This is my job. A well-paid job, I should add. I can't afford to let the opportunity pass. It could be an access pass to much bigger things. Let's say no more about it, yes?'

Jake would normally have argued back. If Granble really was as bad as Abri said, if his diamonds had anything to do with financing wars, then promoting his business was wrong. There was no two ways about it. But his mum looked really upset, so he just nodded.

As they climbed out of the car, the small pocket of protestors was still chanting as they were corralled by security. His mum gathered her things from the boot, looking nervously over towards them.

Now I know what Dad meant by 'look after her'.

While his mum went off to find the models, Jake took his football kit and dashed down to the dressing rooms. He pushed open the door and twenty faces turned to look at him. The entire England squad.

'Hey, it's Little Bastin,' said Mark Fortune, stepping up to shake his hand. 'We weren't sure you'd make it.'

'Thanks for letting me join in,' he said.

'You kidding?' said Fortune. 'When someone like Steve Bastin asks, you don't say no. Go and get your kit on, and let's head out.'

Jake scrambled into his shorts and shirt, and laced up his boots nice and tight, then ran out on to the pitch. Ebner was standing in a tracksuit on the sidelines, holding a ball, which he threw in Jake's path.

'Just a light session today,' he said. 'Big game tomorrow for the boys.'

Cones were lined up widthways across the turf, and the players were dribbling a ball between them to warm up.

Jake's ball skills were always pretty spot on, but he took a bit more care than usual.

No way I'm going to make an idiot of myself by being too clever.

When he'd done a few slaloms, Ebner called them all over for relay shuttles between the halfway line and the D. Jake was surprised how quick some of the team were in the flesh. Especially Ed Francis, the striker. He might not have the best control in top-flight football, but he was like a whippet between the lines. Still, at least Jake was quicker than the defenders. He just about kept pace with Mark Fortune, but by the twentieth shuttle he was panting.

'You're doing really well,' said the midfielder, tossing Jake a water bottle. 'Ebner's a bit of a fitness Nazi, but it's good for the team.'

After that, the assistant coach announced they'd move on to ball drills.

At last, Jake thought. *Some real football*.

Across the pitch, a platform was being wheeled out on to the sidelines. It looked like the sort of thing they used for trophy presentations. When Jake spotted his mum pointing, he realised what it actually was: a catwalk. The Granble logo was daubed on one side.

'My wife won't stop dropping hints,' said Dave Adams,

the England left back. 'She says these Granble stones are supposed to be amazing.'

'I'm gonna get some cufflinks cut with them,' said Robbie Odeji, the winger.

One of the players whistled when a gaggle of models came out. They were struggling with heels in the grass.

'Eyes on the ball, fellas,' said Ebner. 'There'll be time for fun when you retire.'

They played three-on-three, trying to keep the ball from the opposition. It was fast stuff, and Jake got caught on the ball a couple of times by Francis. Mark Fortune showed him a neat trick to draw the ball away and give himself some time, though, and next time Ed came up on him, Jake was able to dummy it away. Francis slid over on to his backside.

'Nice one, Little Bastin,' Robbie said.

The sound of clapping made them all look round. Standing on the sideline, and wearing a short dress showing slashes of bare skin, was Abri.

'Hey, Jake,' she called over. 'You're pretty good.'

All the players looked at him in amazement. He could tell they were itching to say something.

'What is this?!' shouted Ebner. 'Put your tongues away. No drooling on my pitch − it's not good for the turf. Jake, if you want to speak with your girlfriend, give up the ball!'

The players all laughed as Jake trotted off to the sidelines.

'Hi,' he said. 'He didn't mean that, about the girlfriend . . .'

'What?' said Abri. 'You mean you wouldn't want to go out with me?'

'No . . . I . . .' he began.

Her face broke into a wide smile. 'I know what you meant,' she said. 'I was just teasing.'

Jake was sweating a bit anyway, but he felt the blood rush to his cheeks. What was it about this girl that made him a stammering wreck?

'How's it all going?' he asked.

'Boring,' said Abri. 'And hot!' She fanned herself. 'All this make-up in the middle of summer is *not* a good call.'

Jake took the opportunity to inspect her outfit more closely. 'You look good.'

'Why, thank you,' she said. 'Don't know why we need to practise, though. I've been putting one foot in front of the other since I was a year old.'

Jake laughed. Were all supermodels this cool? 'I'm sure there's more to it than that.'

Jake was aware that someone in a pale suit was walking up towards them. The last thing he wanted was an interruption. Not when things were going so well.

'Hi there,' said the man in an American accent. He flicked out his hand, which held a card. 'Randy Freemore, pleased to meet ya.'

Abri gave an amused frown.

'Hello,' said Jake as warmly as he could manage. He took the card. 'Jake Bastin.'

'I know who you are. Let's just say a little bird told me Bastin Junior would be training today.'

Jake hardly knew what to say. Was this guy a scout? He straightened his shoulders. 'I'm just practising with the team,' he said. 'I've not gone pro yet.'

'Really?' said the man. 'Well, that kinda makes you *exactly* what I'm looking for.'

Jake looked at the card. On it was Freemore's name, above the words 'Talent Manager'. The head of the card read: '*Olympic Advantage: Be the Best.*'

'I'll catch you later, Jake,' said Abri, giving a little wave.

'No, wait,' he said. 'I . . .'

'See you at the church with your mum this afternoon. You'll be there, won't you?'

Jake hadn't been planning to, but he changed his plans in an instant.

'I'll be there,' he said.

Abri winked and strode off. Jake watched her for longer

than he should have, then turned his attention back to the smooth-talking American.

'What's Olympic Advantage?' he asked.

Freemore smiled. 'I knew you'd be interested. It's a specialist training camp, based in Florida. Starts in a month's time. We get the best young amateur athletes from around the world, bring 'em to the States, then give 'em a two-week intensive course in physical education. They train with others in their chosen sport, then cross-train with world-class athletes from other disciplines. The idea is to establish ourselves as the stable of the sporting future. We take control of everything – sleep patterns, diet, training. Kind of a one-stop shop for physical excellence.'

Jake wasn't sure about Freemore, but the camp sounded interesting. If his parents wouldn't help him become a professional footballer, maybe this was the next best thing.

'Let me think about it,' he said.

'Sure,' said Freemore, clicking his tongue. 'But don't think too long, kid.'

The sound of the tannoy split the air.

'Extra security to pitch-side immediately.'

Jake and the players all looked to the far side of the pitch. A crowd of around thirty people were climbing from one of the tunnels over the top of the seats. They made it down to the advertising hoardings and scrambled over. Even from a hundred metres away, Jake could make out the T-shirts he'd seen in the car park, bearing anti-Granble slogans. A few of the protestors wielded pieces of wood. One swung a crowbar. Another had ripped up a chair and held it above his head. A dozen security guards came streaming out of the players' tunnel and threw themselves into the onrushing mob, and Jake saw one protestor brutally punched until he keeled over. But it wasn't enough.

The remainder screamed abuse like a war cry as they charged across the pitch towards the catwalk platform. Towards Abri.

And Jake's mother.

9

'**B**ack to the dressing room *now*!' Ebner shouted.

The players began to file off the field, casting confused looks at each other. Not all went, though. Robbie, Price and Mark Fortune came with Jake. They ran towards the catwalk where his mum and the models were sitting ducks up on the runway.

'Slow down the protestors,' Jake shouted. 'I'll get the others to safety.'

Granble's people were standing around looking profession-ally useless, and Jake even noticed the Granble reps from the church scurrying off down the tunnel.

More security came out to face the charge along with the players, but Jake could see it still wouldn't be enough. They met in a scrum near the centre circle.

Jake remembered what his mum had said about this group – the lengths to which they were willing to go. He sprinted up to where the wheeled runway jutted out from the tunnel. Abri, Sienna and Monique were already pushing it around sideways on and Jake threw his weight into it too. Together they tipped the structure over. It crashed on to the turf, forming a barrier between the tunnel and the pitch.

'Climb over,' shouted Jake.

Monique went first, scrambling up the platform and heaving herself over the top. Then Sienna.

There was a shout behind as two of the protestors came running through the melee in the centre circle.

'Diamond thieves!' one shouted. Jake saw that he had some sort of metal piping in his hand, and a wild look in his eyes that said he wouldn't hesitate to use it. As Jake went forwards to meet him, his mother screamed.

'Jake, no!'

The man lifted the pipe but Jake rammed into him before he could swing, charging with his shoulder. They went down together, and Jake pressed his forearm into the attacker's face. He howled. The second one ran on, and Jake scrambled up just in time to see Abri drive a foot into his groin. With a cry of agony, the protestor fell into the upturned flooring of the catwalk, and curled into a ball.

Sienna and Monique pulled Jake's mum to safety behind the overturned platform. A few more protestors had broken through, and were approaching fast. Their eyes were crazed with anger.

'Abri, get over!' said Jake, picking up the piping dropped by the other protestor.

'You first,' she said.

Jake looked at her in amazement. This girl had guts!

'We'll go together,' he said. Jake hurled the pipe towards their attackers, who ducked out of the way. It gave them enough time to scramble over the other side of the platform barricade.

'Is everyone OK?' Jake asked. A glass bottle flew over the top and smashed on the artificial turf that lined the tunnel. Suddenly there were hands and feet pounding the other side. Someone appeared at the far end, trying to climb over.

Jake rushed at him, and pushed him back. The man fell with a cry.

'Get down the tunnel,' Jake said. 'Find help.'

The crack of a gunshot brought silence.

Everyone froze. Jake stared at his mother in horror.

She was pale. 'What happened? Has someone been shot?'

'It was probably just a warning,' said Jake, hoping he was right.

He pulled himself up to look over their self-made barrier. Armed security guards were shepherding the protestors into the centre circle at gunpoint. No one was resisting any more. And there was no sign of anyone badly injured.

Mark Fortune and the other players who'd stayed on the pitch to help were now standing well back on the far side of the pitch with the assistant coach. They'd done a brave thing coming out to stop the protestors.

'It looks like everything's calmed down,' Jake said, sliding back to join his mother and the models.

'You saved us,' Abri said, slipping her arm around him.

'You saved yourselves,' he replied. 'I just helped.' He drummed his hand on the wooden surface of the catwalk. 'That was quick thinking to turn this over. Stopped them getting behind the stands, wreaking more havoc.'

'Guess we're more than just pretty faces,' Sienna said sarcastically.

Jake heard footsteps pounding down the tunnel. His pulse quickened. Was it more protestors? Then he saw who it was. His dad – moving so fast, he'd forgotten he faked a limp.

'Jake! Hayley! Are you all right?' he called, gasping for breath. 'God, I saw it from the commentary box.'

He wrapped Jake's mum in his arms and she pressed her head into his chest. After the businesslike kiss at the airport, the sudden show of affection knocked Jake off-balance.

'It's lucky Jake was here,' said Abri. 'We'd have been caught up in the worst, otherwise.'

His dad nodded gravely at him. The look wasn't much, but Jake knew what it meant: *You did well*.

'Hay,' said his dad. 'You could have been seriously hurt. This has to stop, don't you think? Time to sit it out.'

Jake's mother pulled away, disentangling herself. 'Just because of this?'

Jake's dad shrugged. 'It's risky. These people are serious.'

'It'll take more than a few protestors to stop the Granble shoot,' Jake's mum said.

His dad tried to reach for her arm. 'Hay, I care about you –'

She shook him off.

'I can look after myself, Steve.'

Jake could feel a fight brewing. *Did they have to do this in front of Abri?*

'All I'm saying,' said his dad, 'is that there'll be other assignments. Safer ones.'

Jake saw blood rushing to his mum's face, but she held it together.

'I'll be careful,' she said. 'I know what I'm doing.'

Jake's dad looked at the ground, his shoulders sagging.

I guess now's not the time to mention Olympic Advantage, Jake thought to himself.

A painful silence descended, until Steve turned round and trudged back up the tunnel. A few moments later, his mum followed.

'Sorry about that,' Jake said to Abri. 'My parents don't really get on.'

'Don't worry about it,' she said. 'That's life. It's worse for you, stuck in the middle.'

You don't know the half of it, Jake thought.

10

Jake's mum drove to the church more slowly this time. He thought she must still be in shock.

'Maybe you should listen to Dad,' Jake said. 'Granble can find another photographer, can't he?' He rushed to add, 'Not as good as you, obviously.'

'Reputation counts for everything in this business, Jake. You quit one job, prove yourself unreliable, no one will hire you again.'

Jake dropped it.

'Anyway,' his mum continued, smiling, 'enough about me. You and Abri seem to be getting on pretty well.' Jake felt his cheeks redden. 'And from that blush, I'm guessing you quite like her.'

Jake rolled down the window. 'I'll do you a deal, Mum. I won't mention Granble, if you don't mention Abri.'

'Sounds fair,' she said, laughing to herself. 'But what

shall we talk about?'

This is my chance, Jake thought.

He fished Randy Freemore's card out of his pocket. 'Have you heard of Olympic Advantage?'

'Nope.'

Jake went on to explain how Mr Freemore had been at the San Siro, and had given him the card. 'It's like a camp for athletes of the future, in Florida. Really intensive − they teach you everything.' Jake was getting excited just talking about it. 'Not just the sport itself, but lifestyle, nutrition, physio . . .'

'A football camp?' interrupted his mum.

'Yes, sort of, but so much more . . .'

'In *Florida*?' She said the word like it was the moon, or something. Jake could see from her frown that she didn't share his enthusiasm.

'What's wrong, Mum?'

They'd reached the church and she pulled up outside, killed the engine and looked straight at Jake.

'I'm not sure I'm happy about you heading so far on your own.'

'I won't be on my own. There'll be other players, from all over the world . . .'

'That's what I'm worried about,' she said. 'Football's big business. Everyone wants a piece of the pie. I'm not sure I want *you* being that pie, Jake.'

'Mum, what are you talking about? This is a chance of a lifetime!'

'Let me talk to your dad about it, eh?'

Oh, so you'll work together when you're trying to stop me doing something!

Jake climbed out of the car to let his temper cool. He was afraid of saying something he shouldn't.

There were a few crushed cigarette butts on the ground by the side door of the church, but no sign of Hector or the other electricians. In their place stood two security guards in polo-necks and pale blazers. If they had guns, they were hidden. They eyeballed Jake and his mother as they approached. Jake wondered why they weren't watching the front door, but he guessed it was probably bolted shut. One way in, one way out. Easy to guard.

They were waved inside.

Jake was immediately disappointed: no sign of Abri or the other models. Jake couldn't see Granble anywhere, but there were plenty of his lackeys rushing around, and his chief goon, Jaap, stood motionless, still handcuffed to the briefcase.

One hundred million dollars worth of diamonds was a lot to lose.

'Let's get started, shall we?' said his mum. Jake hung back out of the way, while she unpacked her camera and rearranged the supplementary lighting and screens near the altar. Jaap came forwards with the case, fiddled with the code and clicked it open. Jake, along with everyone else, found himself stepping closer to see.

Marissa stepped forwards, and took off what looked like a protective cover.

A collective gasp sounded across the sanctuary.

Jake had seen diamonds before, in jewellery shop windows, and on wedding rings, but nothing compared to the contents of the case. These weren't even rocks – they were *boulders*!

The case was lined with black velvet. Laid out against it was a necklace strung from stones the size of Jake's thumbnail and bracelets made with hundreds of delicate diamonds. Other smaller pieces surrounded a stone as big as Jake's palm.

He didn't even know diamonds came that big.

'Move away, please,' said Marissa.

As people fell back, she donned a pair of white cloth gloves, like a surgeon about to perform an operation. She took out the necklace and placed it carefully against the black altar cloth.

Slowly the room returned to normal. Jake heard the soft

electrical clicks of his mother's camera as she took shots from different angles, at one point standing on a pew to get a better vantage. After each position, she'd consult Marissa, who seemed to be ticking things off on a list. They whispered to each other, as though there was a real church service going on.

Jake was soon bored, and the pew was uncomfortable. When would Abri get here? At least then he'd have someone to talk to. His mum was looking at the viewfinder, going back over old shots, while Jake fingered the Olympic Advantage card.

He'd have to make sure he spoke to his dad before his mum had a chance. If anyone would understand what this meant to Jake, it would be his dad. He'd have to stress all the positives – the structured tuition, the responsible coaches, the healthy elements – it was a chance to grow as a person as well as a player blah, blah, blah . . .

His mum leant closer to the diamonds and took a few more quick shots. Suddenly, Jake was aware of the quickstep of heels on stone behind him.

'Stop that!' shouted Marissa. 'No, no, no!'

Granble's assistant rushed past Jake with Jaap just behind her, while Jake's mum straightened up, a look of alarm on her face. 'What is it?'

Marissa tapped the clipboard and turned it to face his mum.

'Only the shots on the approved list, remember?' she shouted. 'Jaap, delete them.'

The henchman stepped forwards and reached for the camera. Jake's mum pulled it out of the way. 'Hey!'

Jake was up in a second and at his mother's side.

'You can't do that!' he said.

Marissa looked at him with a curl of her lip, then addressed his mum.

'Miss Maguire, do I need to remind you of my employer's very strict instructions? There are to be no close-ups of the diamonds under any circumstances. If you cannot stick to the stipulations in the contract – or keep your son under control – I'm sure Mr Granble will see that contract terminated forthwith.'

Jake's mum relaxed and unlooped the camera strap from her neck. Jaap unceremoniously snatched it from her hand and began deleting the photos. When he handed it back, Jake stepped up to him, nose to nose.

'You shouldn't be so rough,' he said.

Jaap didn't say anything. His glance flicked to Marissa, and in his peripheral vision Jake saw her give a tiny shake of her head. Jaap backed away.

'That's enough, Jake,' said his mum, putting a hand on

his arm. 'It was just a misunderstanding. Let's carry on with the shoot.'

'Yes, let's,' said Marissa, looking pointedly at Jake, 'but I think we should get rid of any *non-essential* personnel, don't you?'

'Honey,' said his mum, 'why don't you see if you can get any further with my broken camera? It's in the car. You've got your laptop now too.'

Jake could hear the note of stress in his mum's voice. She didn't need a hero. She had never put up with his dad's overprotectiveness, either.

'Sure, Mum,' said Jake. 'I could do with some fresh air.'

He went outside, letting his anger cool, and opened the boot. Inside he found the damaged camera and his laptop. Now he needed somewhere to work, away from the glaring eyes of Granble's goons.

Jake did a quick circuit of the church. He passed the church's main doors, two tall timber panels with a smaller door cut away. All locked. Around the far side, a narrow alley led to a metal gate that opened back on to the street. Worth a look. Jake went along the alley. Halfway down, and slightly recessed, was another door, hinged with thick iron embossing. It looked like it had been there for as long as the church. The door had been boarded up but the wood was rotting. One board dangled from a single nail. Jake gave the door a stiff yank and it gave way.

He quickly checked left and right, then went inside. He found himself in a room with a simple table and what looked like the remains of wooden hanging closets, now worm-eaten, lined up side by side. The vestry. He laughed to himself: this was the room where Abri and the others had been changing the other day. He tried not to think about *that* too hard. There was a door back into the main part of the church, and against the opposite wall were a couple of steps leading up to another doorway. Jake crossed quickly and found it was a second entrance to the spiral stairwell, dimly lit through lead-framed windows.

Jake sat on the steps and opened up his laptop, plugging his mum's camera into the USB socket. He found the files and copied them to his hard drive. Since it would take a few minutes to download, Jake thought he'd quickly check on his mum. He went to peer through into the nave. Hayley was still snapping away. Marissa was close by her, watching like a hawk. Jake finally noticed Granble himself, standing in the shadows to one side at the back.

His laptop gave a muted beep – the files had finished copying. Jake closed the door slowly and went back to his computer. He opened a batch of six photos. They were the shots his mum had taken at the airport. There was nothing wrong with them, which meant the electronic files were undamaged. Jake skipped past, embarrassed.

Those were some photos I'd have been happy to lose!

Next were the candids of the models in the street. There were some of them buying coffees, laughing at a joke, sitting on the kerbside. Just like three girlfriends out having fun. Well, three impossibly hot girlfriends. Seeing Abri again made Jake's mouth go a little dry.

There was one shot where she leant against a wall, looking to one side, like she was waiting for someone. Jake couldn't help but zoom in on her face. Perfect bone structure, almond-shaped eyes, lips slightly parted . . .

But then something else caught Jake's eye. Further down the street, in the same shot, Sienna was speaking to someone. A guy, sitting on a moped. He didn't look like a model. Maybe Sienna wasn't as icy as she pretended. The pair were almost out of shot, and slightly blurred. If he hadn't zoomed in, he would have missed them.

There was a noise – a soft *woomf*, and a camera flash came through a crack in the door.

Then a scream cut the air.

11

Jake put down the camera quickly and stood up. He heard raised voices. Shouting in Italian, and his mother's voice, panicked. 'What's happening?'

There was another flash, and the same strange noise, like a muffled explosion.

Jake ran to the door and put his eye to the crack. If there was one thing St Petersburg had taught him, it was to assess the situation and not run in blindly.

Smoke filled the nave in a billowing cloud. Through the fog, Jake saw his mother lying draped over a pew. Beside her Marissa was on the floor on her back. Granble was on the floor, a hand thrown up over his mouth. Jaap crawled on his hands and knees along the central aisle. Then he, too, collapsed.

Jake ran out into the church, towards his mother's body.

'Mum!' Jake shouted. But something was wrong. The air

scorched his throat and his eyes streamed with tears. His legs felt weak and numb, like he was dragging himself through thick mud.

Ten metres short of his mother, Jake tripped, and put out his hand to stop himself. His brain felt like a wet sponge, his head spun with dizziness and he thought he was going to be sick. He fell sideways, and his head thumped into the cold stone. He fought to keep his eyes open, but he couldn't lift his neck.

Stay awake, Bastin.

As he lay there trying not to breath, two figures appeared through the smoke. They were dressed in black fatigues, and wore gas masks. They moved among the bodies steadily. Jake wasn't sure if he was dreaming. The burn in his throat was getting worse, his brain feeling wetter.

The guys from the airport. It has to be.

The figures reached the altar. One held open some sort of drawstring purse, while the other swept the diamonds inside. They helped themselves to the pieces still in the case. It took less than ten seconds and with a nod to each other the black-clad figures swept out again. Jake couldn't keep his eyes open any longer.

The world went black.

*

'Jake! Jake, baby. Wake up!'

The room was spinning. Shadows moved above him. *Voices.*

Jake opened his eyes. His mother was crouched over him, her hair a mess.

'Mum?'

Her face broke into a weak smile. Jake tried to push himself up on to his elbows, but slumped back. He felt a pain on his head and reached to feel it. Blood. He'd opened up his scab from Russia.

'Are you OK, Mum?'

'I think so, but take it easy. They used some sort of stun grenades. Poison gas.'

Jake tried to get up again, but his head swooned. He fell back down with a thud. He looked at his mum. The smoke had cleared all but the upper reaches of the church.

'It was a professional job,' Jake said. 'They had masks.'

'You saw them?' snapped a man. It was Jaap. He pushed one of the lighting assistants aside, and looked down at Jake. 'How many?'

'Two,' said Jake.

'Impossible,' said Jaap. 'I had my best men on the entrance.'

'I'm telling you what I saw,' said Jake. He used a palm flat on the floor to steady himself and Hayley helped him get to his feet. 'They took the diamonds?'

His mum nodded. 'Luckily, no one seems to have been seriously hurt.'

Jaap, looking white with fury, snorted. Clearly he would have traded the lives of everyone in the church for those stones.

They made their way outside into the sun. One of the security guards was holding a bloodied shirt to the side of his head, the other was drinking from a water bottle with a shaky hand. Jaap snapped at them in Afrikaans, and they mumbled words of what Jake guessed were apology.

What the hell just happened?

He suddenly felt angry. *Had his dad suspected something like this might happen? Is that why he'd pawned him off on his mum the moment they hit Milan?*

Granble was on the phone, pacing back and forth. He was speaking urgently, and didn't seem to care if anyone heard. 'This is a temporary setback, I tell you . . . No, there's no need for that, not yet . . . It must have been an inside job . . . That's right, a leak . . . My top people . . . Who else? Well, the models, the photographer, of course . . .'

Jake realised that Jaap was glaring at him. The thug sidled over.

'Where did you come from?' he snarled. 'You were supposed to be outside the church.'

'I was in the old vestry,' said Jake coldly. 'I heard a scream, but when I came in everyone was already out cold.'

'Very convenient!' Jaap said. 'Can you prove it?'

Jake felt his fists curling into balls. The South African had the look of a brawler, with a caved nose that had been broken at least once.

I'll be happy to break it for you again, thought Jake.

His mum stepped between them. 'That's enough!'

Jaap stepped away with a snarl to Granble's side, and Jake's mum pulled him away to the car.

'Jake, you need to get a hold of your temper. *Everyone's* upset about this.'

'He's pushing me,' Jake said. 'How could anyone think I had something to do with this?'

A taxi pulled up. Abri, Sienna and Monique climbed out. When they saw everyone outside, Abri walked to Jake and his mum with an uncertain smile on her face. 'What's going on?'

'There's been a robbery,' Jake's mum said. 'Someone's stolen Granble's diamonds.'

'What?' she said. 'That's crazy! Are you OK?'

'They used gas to knock everyone out,' said Jake.

He nodded to the security guards. 'Looks like they used something harder on the doormen.'

'What about the shoot?' said Sienna.

Jake's mum shrugged. She looked defeated. 'No diamonds, no shoot, I guess.'

'And the runway show?' asked Monique.

'It's tomorrow,' Jake's mum said. 'So either we recover the diamonds, or get replacements. If not, the whole launch will have to be cancelled.'

'Have you phoned the police?' asked Abri.

'No police!' Granble barked. 'This is our problem, and we'll deal with it our way.'

'But, Mr Granble, sir,' Jake's mum said. 'This is a massive diamond heist. Someone could have been badly hurt. Surely you . . .'

'Did you not hear me, Miss Maguire? I said that I do not want the police involved. My diamonds and my staff are *my* business. *Capito?*'

'I understand,' said Jake's mum, cowed. Jake hated seeing her act like that.

'Arse,' he said, under his breath, as Granble stormed off.

Abri laughed, but his mum didn't.

'Maybe you should go back to your dad's for a while, Jake,' she said sternly.

It wasn't a suggestion. Jake was about to say he didn't need a babysitter, but he could see the worry in his mum's eyes.

She's been through a lot today.

'Sure, Mum,' he said. 'Will you be OK on your own?'

Granble was shouting into his phone again. 'I told you, there's no need for that! I can fix this, but you need to give me time . . .'

'I have to speak with Mr Granble for a while. It sounds like his investors are on his back already. We need to figure out how we can salvage the shoot and the runway show tomorrow.'

'He's got a short fuse,' said Jake.

'Takes one to know one,' said his mother with a grin. 'If only it was as simple as taking a few pictures.'

That reminded him. 'I got your pictures downloaded, by the way. They're fine. Camera's knackered, though.'

'That's great, Jake,' said his mum, looking at Granble. He could see his mum's mind was elsewhere already.

'I'll just grab my stuff from the vestry,' he said.

'I'll come with you,' Abri said. Jake thought he saw Sienna roll her eyes.

Abri and Jake went back into the church. It was weirdly silent now. Hard to think that less than half an hour ago it had been the scene of such chaos.

In the vestry, he unplugged the camera and gathered his stuff.

'You must be pretty good with computers,' said Abri. 'I thought the pictures were lost.'

'It wasn't a big problem,' Jake said, trying not to sound too boastful. 'Just a hardware fault. There are some really good ones of you three in the street.'

'Really?' Abri smiled. 'I'd like to see them some time.'

She was biting her lip again. Was she really talking about photos, or was there some kind of hidden code going on? Jake found it hard to tear his eyes away. 'Sure, whenever's good for you.'

On their way out of the church, Jaap and the security guard with the cut to his head blocked the way.

'We need to frisk you,' he said. 'Make sure nothing contraband's coming out of that church.'

'This is ridiculous,' said Jake. 'I already told you –'

'Don't worry,' said Abri. 'They're just taking precautions – aren't you, gentlemen?'

Jaap nodded and narrowed his eyes as though he wasn't sure whether she was making fun or not.

Jake lifted his arms while the guard patted him down. Jaap did Abri.

Probably enjoying it too, Jake thought. He fought

down the urge to shove the pervert off her.

'Now, hand over the computer,' said Jaap.

Jake looked at him in astonishment. 'It's *my* property.'

Jaap nodded at his colleague, who moved quickly and pinned Jake's arms. 'Get off me!' Jake shouted. The computer was prised from his grip and he was pushed back out into the churchyard.

'And your handbag, miss,' said Jaap. 'You'll get it all back when we've done a thorough search.'

Abri handed it over. 'It's this season,' she said, a hint of warning in her voice.

Jake was still seething when he met his mum again. She scanned him up and down. 'Where's your computer?'

Jake gestured over his shoulder. 'Ask your control-freak boss.'

His mum cast another anxious glance towards Granble. 'I ordered you a taxi,' she said. 'It'll drop the girls off first, then take you back to your dad's hotel.'

Five minutes later, the cab arrived and they climbed in. Monique sat up front with the driver and Jake was wedged between Abri and Sienna in the back seat. The taxi drove off, leaving his mum standing alone in front of the old church. Jake twisted in his seat, keeping his eyes on her, but his last view was Jaap watching them from the side door.

'You're worried about her, aren't you?' Abri asked.

Jake nodded, straightening in his seat. It could very easily have been his mother's blood in the church aisle, not his own.

'I don't want her to get hurt,' said Jake. 'This job means so much to her that I think she's losing perspective.'

'It sounds like these thieves were professionals,' said Abri. She placed her hand on his leg. 'They wouldn't hurt innocent people.'

'Not unless it was *necessary*,' Sienna added, unhelpfully.

Jake smiled to show he appreciated their words. He wasn't angry about the robbery. If anything, he had a grudging respect for the thieves. They'd lifted a hundred million dollars from under Granble's nose in a matter of minutes. That was impressive.

No, his mind was taking him somewhere else.

A job like that took meticulous planning. It needed brains as well as brawn. The thieves must have gathered quite a bit of intelligence before attempting such an act. Not to mention the fact that they'd used military grenades as part of their operation. Were they part of the same group who'd protested at the stadium? They seemed more organised than that. Another question pushed itself to the front of Jake's mind – something he'd wondered before, but was now beginning to fixate on:

Is this the real reason Dad and I came to Milan?

12

'Via San Martino,' said the driver.

They pulled up to the kerb next to a tall block of flats.

'Hardly the Hilton, is it?' Abri said.

'Why are you staying *here*?' Jake asked.

'Sometimes it's better to be away from the paparazzi,' Abri said. Monique was already out of the car.

'Come on, Abri, we need to go.' Sienna exited the car. The driver gave an annoyed glance over his shoulder.

'Sorry, Jake,' Abri said, resting her hand on Jake's. 'Jaap took our handbags. We don't have any money.'

'It's fine,' he said. 'I'll pay when I get back to mine.'

Jake thought he heard Sienna mutter something about Abri's boy before she slammed the car door. He was really starting to dislike her.

'Well, thank you,' said Abri, giving him a peck on the cheek. 'And thanks for seeing us back safely.'

Monique and Sienna were crossing the street towards the door of the apartment block.

'You're not back safe yet,' Jake said. 'Wave when you get upstairs.'

'We can take care of ourselves, you know,' Abri said.

'I know,' Jake replied. 'But give me a wave anyway.'

'OK,' said Abri, climbing out. 'We're on the fifth floor. Watch out.'

Jake watched her follow the other two. Sienna was shaking her head, and had a serious look. What was her problem?

'*Dov'e?*' asked the driver. Where to?

'*Uno momento,*' Jake replied. He scanned the building. In less than two minutes, a window opened on to a Juliet balcony and Abri leant out. She blew a kiss. It made Jake realise he was blushing.

The driver nodded, and gave Jake a little grin that didn't need a translator: *Lucky you.*

Jake grinned back and lifted his eyebrows: *I know.*

Fifteen minutes later, the driver pulled up outside his dad's place. Jake paid the driver and took the lift up to the ninth floor. As it rose towards the penthouse, Jake started to forget about Abri and started thinking about the theft again. Twice in one day his mum could have been harmed, and he was sure his dad knew something he wasn't letting on.

Him and his secrets! I thought we'd left all that behind in Russia.

They were supposed to be a team now.

Instead of opening, the keypad on the inside of the lift flashed, asking for a four-digit access code. He was about to ring his dad to ask when he thought he might guess instead. He keyed 0909. His dad scored his first goal for Tottenham Hotspur on 9 September 1985. The doors swished open.

Sometimes even Steve Bastin was predictable.

The doors opened right into the suite. The living area floor was laminate wood with thick rugs, and a massive L-shaped sofa faced a flat-screen telly and a free-standing fireplace with a chimney that funnelled up into the roof space. A kitchen on the other side was fairly small and functional, while there was a corridor leading off towards three doors. Jake guessed a couple of bedrooms and a bathroom. The opposite side of the lounge was green-tinted glass, tilted at an angle. Jake saw his dad on the roof terrace beyond, sitting on a chair. He had his top off and was tapping away on a laptop, with a bottle of Evian on the table next to him.

When he saw Jake, he stood up and came inside. Despite being in his mid-forties, his dad was in good shape, and went to the gym four or five times a week. Jake had always thought it was a hang-up from his playing days, but now he knew different. His dad needed to stay fit for his job.

'Hayley called ahead,' said his dad. 'I'm glad you're both OK. If you hadn't been there –'

Jake wasn't in the mood to waste any more time. 'What's going on, Dad?'

The question took his dad by surprise. He put his finger to his lips, and pointed outside, scooping up his iPhone as he walked. Jake followed him on to the terrace. There hadn't been any wind at street level, but up here gusts whipped the small conifers in the plant boxes. His dad leant over the railings.

Beside him, Jake couldn't help but admire the view. The gothic spires of the cathedral, half-built office skyscrapers in the distance – old and new all mixed in together.

'Can't be too careful inside,' his dad said.

'You think it's bugged?' said Jake.

'Always assume the worst.'

'So you're going to answer my question? You knew she'd be in danger, didn't you?'

His dad shook his head. 'You have to believe me, Jake. I didn't know about the robbery until Hayley phoned me.'

'Why should I believe you?'

'I wouldn't have put you in harm's way,' said his dad. 'Either of you.'

'But you knew *something* might happen!'

'Keep your voice down,' said his dad, 'and I'll tell you.'

Jake calmed himself. 'Go on, then.'

His dad took a sip of water. 'The commentary job's a cover. Granble's the real reason I'm here. The Granble Diamond Company may look legit on paper, but my superiors have their doubts. Our operatives in South Africa think that a lot of his mining practices are illegal, and that he's trading in blood diamonds.'

'What's that got to do with the security services?' Jake asked. 'Not being funny, but where's the threat to Britain?'

'It's not quite that simple,' said his dad. 'It's where the money ends up that's the problem. Arms, terrorism, extremists – issues that *will* threaten innocent people, all over the world. MI6 is just one cog in a machine trying to stop it.'

Jake gave a low whistle. 'Why didn't you tell me this before? I could have helped.'

His dad pursed his lips. 'I have my orders too.'

'But I thought after Russia –'

'Look, Jake,' his dad interrupted. 'This business is all about information and trust. You pass the information to people you trust, and you buy trust with information. My superiors have never even met you.'

It frustrated Jake, but he understood. 'So why are you telling me now?'

His dad gave him a playful shove. 'Because *I* trust you and someone's raised the stakes.'

'Does Mum know anything about this?'

His dad shook his head. 'No, and she mustn't. We have to keep our cover. If Granble suspects we're on to him, he'll pull up the drawbridge.'

'But if Mum's in danger –'

'She'll be in *more* danger if she starts acting strangely. I need you to stay close to her. You saw how she was at the stadium – she doesn't want me interfering.'

'So what *will* you be doing?' Jake asked.

'Acting like a commentator,' said his dad. 'My brief is to gather what intel I can, and get close to Granble. I've already met Granble once at the stadium, and there's another event planned after the game tomorrow night.'

'But the launch can't go ahead now,' Jake said. 'The diamonds are gone.'

'That suits me,' replied his father. 'Hayley won't have to have anything else to do with him. Until then, I need you to stay sharp.'

'You got it,' said Jake. 'I'll be able to look for anything suspicious too. Granble thinks I'm just an annoying kid.'

Jake's dad stood back from the balcony, and pointed his finger at Jake's chest. 'Don't start acting on your own initiative,' he said. 'Observe and report, nothing more.'

'Chill out, Dad, I won't do anything to raise suspicions.'

'Just like with the minister, you mean?'

'I learned my lesson.'

'Good,' said his dad. He started walking back inside. 'I need to clean up for a gala dinner later. It's a tux job.'

Jake watched his dad go in, and turned back to look over the balcony. The city shimmered in the late afternoon heat. Thousands of people milled about, seeing the sites, leaving their jobs for the day. And amongst them two people had a hundred million dollars worth of stolen diamonds.

Jake planned to find out who.

13

Jake fixed himself a sandwich and watched the Germany–Spain game highlights on the TV in the penthouse suite. The Germans were stifling the creative play of the Spanish, and it was actually one of the more boring games Jake had seen in his life.

The doorbell chimed just after six, and Jake's dad shouted through from the bedroom for Jake to get it.

A squat Italian was looking into the videocom.

'*Taxi per il Signor Bastin,*' he said.

'He'll be down in a minute,' said Jake.

His dad emerged along the corridor wearing an immaculate dinner jacket, crisp white dress shirt and black tie.

'Can I mix you a vodka Martini, Mr Bond?' Jake joked.

'Ha ha,' said his dad, tugging at his collar. 'James Bond? I look more like a penguin.'

Jake reached for the remote control to turn off the TV.

'Oooh, what's the score?' his dad asked.

'Nil−nil,' Jake replied. 'Don't watch, unless you want to fall asleep and miss the party.'

'Doesn't sound like a bad alternative.'

'Can you give me a ride back over to Mum's on the way?'

'Sure.'

They climbed into the lift together. As it descended, his dad fiddled with his cufflinks. 'By the way, I got a call from an American gentleman this afternoon. Randy something . . .'

'Olympic Advantage?' Jake asked.

'That's right,' his dad said. 'It sounds like a great opportunity.'

Jake felt like punching the air, but kept his cool. Obviously his mum hadn't mentioned her feelings on the matter yet.

'It's amazing, Dad,' he said. 'I checked it out online. The equipment and facilities are state of the art. And it's in the summer, so I wouldn't miss any school −'

'Hold up!' said his dad. 'You don't have to give me the spiel. I got that already from this guy.'

'And you think it's a good idea?' said Jake.

The lift doors swished open on the ground floor.

'It *sounds* promising, but I want to do some more research first.'

Jake grinned, and pushed his worries to the back of his

mind. So what if his mum wasn't so keen? His dad sounded persuadable.

There were *some* advantages to having divorced parents.

Next morning, Jake sat on the sofa reading the news online. Granble's security people had turned his computer over to his mum the day before. He'd done a quick scan of it and was relieved to see that Granble's people hadn't messed with anything. All his mum's photos were still safely copied on to the hard drive.

There was nothing at all about the jewel heist in the news. Complete media blackout. Granble must have good PR people to keep a story like that out of the press.

Well, he had Marissa. She could probably keep a fox out of a hen house.

'I appreciate that,' said Hayley into her mobile, 'but I just want to know where things stand for tonight.'

It seemed to Jake that his mum had been on the phone since seven that morning dealing with the fallout from the theft the day before.

'But there will still be a show, right?' said his mum.

Whatever answer Marissa gave, it wasn't the one his mum wanted to hear. She sighed, and rubbed her temples. 'I understand, but please just keep me informed.'

She closed the phone.

'Any news?' said Jake.

'What do you think?' his mum snapped. She sat down heavily beside his feet at the end of the sofa. 'Sorry, Jake, I didn't mean to take it out on you.'

'That's OK, Mum,' said Jake, shifting closer to her. 'I know how important this was to you. Is the show going ahead?'

His mum nodded. 'So far, yes. But without the diamonds it'll be a disaster. Mr Granble seems convinced we'll get them back.'

Something about those last words made Jake nervous. Granble didn't seem like the sort of man who let those who crossed him get away with it. Jake hated sitting around when he could be helping solve the crime. He was the only one who had seen the assailants after all.

His mum's phone started ringing again, and she answered: 'Hayley Maguire . . . Oh, hi, Stefan . . . No, nothing yet . . .'

Jake assured himself that his mum was safe for the moment, stuck at home waiting by the phone. He got up off the sofa and pointed towards the door. He mouthed, 'Going to see Dad.'

His mum waved goodbye.

It was good to get out, but Jake had no intention of going to see his dad. He had a plan, which was only a little beyond his dad's instructions to observe and report. He needed more information and he knew just the person he wanted to see.

He took a cab back to Abri's place on Via San Martino, stopping on the way at a florist's. After a couple of minutes looking aimlessly at the various flowers, the owner – a stout, middle-aged lady with chaotic black hair – came up to him. 'English, *si*?'

Was it that obvious? '*Si*. I need to buy some flowers.' Jake cringed at his attempt to mime along with his words.

'For *girl*, I think?' said the owner, a sly smile splitting her face.

Jake nodded. He could feel the taxi driver watching him – probably with a matching smile.

Shortly after, he left the shop with a large bunch of orange and violet flowers.

Time for a charm offensive!

Abri was the only one who'd dared to speak out against Granble at the church, and if she knew something that might help the case against the tycoon, then Jake wanted to be the one to hand over that information.

He rang the buzzer, a smile creeping over his face.

And if he had to interview three beautiful models to get that information . . .

It was a hard job, but someone had to do it.

No one picked up. That was weird. He checked his watch. 11 a.m. Surely the girls wouldn't have left for the stadium yet? Nor would they be out for lunch. They could still be asleep. Maybe it was true about supermodels not getting out of bed for less than ten thousand dollars.

Jake shielded his eyes and peered in the slim window that ran down one side of the door. He could see a large entry way with a staircase at one side. Jake was about to ring again, when a burly-looking Italian in sunglasses with a bad buzz-cut appeared at the top of the staircase and bolted down the stairs. Jake had to step aside quickly as the man shoved the front door open and pushed past. Jake stuck his toe against the jamb to prevent it closing.

I guess I'll surprise them, he thought.

Jake waited until the man had ducked into a dark sedan across the street before he slipped into the building and headed for the stairs. Five floors was good exercise – and it would give him time to fine tune his opening line.

Hi, Abri, I was just passing by . . .

Hey, I got these for you . . .

How's it going, Abri?

Jake stepped out through a door marked *Ap. 500–540*. He tried to remember which window Abri had waved from. It was five windows along in his mind's eye, so apartment 510.

He knocked on the door. He heard noises inside, then a few seconds later a middle-aged woman in a dressing gown with rollers in her hair opened the door.

'*Si?*' she said.

'I'm sorry,' said Jake, confused. '*Mi dispiace*. Abri?'

The woman looked at him like he was from Mars, then slammed the door.

Jake looked each way along the corridor. *I'm sure this is right.*

He wandered back to the stairs, then realised his mistake. He was on the fourth floor! The ground floor must be labelled 100–140, the first floor 200–240 ...

What had his dad said about staying sharp?

So busy practising your chat-up lines you forgot to count. Moron.

Jake took another flight of stairs up, and went along to Abri's flat. The door to 610 was open an inch. Not too security conscious, these girls. He knocked anyway.

No answer. Jake pushed the door. 'Hello? It's me, Jake.'

The door opened a foot then hit an obstruction.

Jake pushed his head through the crack to see what was blocking it. On the floor lay a body, face down. From the blonde hair, Jake knew it was Sienna.

He dropped the flowers, squeezed into the flat and

crouched beside her. His first thought was overdose. There were always stories in the papers about models taking drugs.

'Sienna?' he said, reaching for her shoulder. She didn't react.

Jake carefully turned her over and nearly choked with shock. Sienna's face was deadly pale, her eyes open and bloodshot. Her tongue, almost as purple as the flowers, was hanging out of the corner of her mouth. But it was the red line across her neck that made his heart thump. Something had been pulled tight across her throat, breaking the skin.

This was no overdose.

It was murder.

14

Jake checked for a pulse, knowing already that it was pointless.

Sienna's wrist was limp, but still warm. He felt his stomach turn with fear.

Whoever did this is close.

Then his mind cleared and a thought pierced him like a needle: *The others!*

'Abri!' Jake called out. 'Abri! Monique!'

He ran along the hall. Two bedrooms, empty but ransacked. Drawers upturned, sheets and mattresses ripped up, a mirror smashed on the floor. In the bathroom, a medicine cabinet had been wrenched off the wall, and a perfume bottle shattered, leaving the air heavy with sweetness. The bath panel had been removed. It was the same story in the lounge and small open-plan kitchen. Deserted, but demolished. Someone had been looking for something – something that they were willing to kill for.

Jake felt a blast of relief. Abri wasn't here and he hoped that meant she was safe.

He heard a door creak and picked up a leg from a broken chair. The wood felt heavy in his palm, but he was ready to use it. Then a scream came from the hallway. Jake rushed back into the corridor.

Abri was standing over Sienna's body, her hands covering her mouth, trembling. She looked up at Jake, her eyes settling on the makeshift club in his hand.

'What have you done?' she screamed.

'It's not how it looks,' he said. 'I found her –'

He didn't get a chance to finish. With a howl of anger, Abri lunged over Sienna's corpse. Jake thought she was going to kick him, but her foot went behind his and she slammed an open palm into Jake's solar plexus. He fell back, dropping the weapon, and rolled over on the varnished floor. Abri lifted her heel and axe-kicked down towards his head. Jake rolled sideways into the wall as her stiletto snapped off with the force of the blow.

She hobbled back and he sprang up.

'No!' he said, moving forwards to stifle any further blows. 'You've got it wrong.'

Abri lurched in, grabbed his hand and twisted him over

her hip in a judo throw. Jake could do nothing as the world turned over and he thumped on to his back. Abri kept a grip of his arm and tried to twist it upwards. Jake rolled with the hold and shoved her away. A second later she would have snapped his arm at the elbow.

This girl knows how to fight.

Abri grabbed the chair leg. 'How could you?' she hissed.

'She was dead when I got here,' Jake replied, gasping for breath from the hard landing.

'You expect me to believe that?' she said, lunging at him, stabbing with the club. Jake fell back. As she flicked a lightning roundhouse kick towards his head, he caught her foot. Abri simply turned and rolled away, pulling her foot free. Jake was left holding her other shoe.

'I don't want to hurt you,' he said. 'Just listen to me.'

Abri gave a barked laugh, and threw the chair leg. Jake blocked with a hand and it clattered behind him. There were no more weapons to hand, but Jake didn't fancy his chances anyway. If he didn't get out, this was going to end really badly for one of them. And it looked like it was going to be him.

He stepped backwards until he was through the flat's front door. He tripped over the bouquet he'd brought Abri as he stumbled into the main corridor. Abri came after him, with hate in her eyes. 'No way,' she said. 'You're not going anywhere!'

Jake ran towards the stairwell. Abri was right behind him. He took the stairs three at a time, using the banister for balance. Down half a flight, he saw Abri vault the handrail, and flip through the air, landing nimbly one flight down on the landing.

Wait a minute . . .

He stopped.

He'd seen that move before.

Jake struggled to understand. He jumped the remaining steps. Abri caught his cheek with a hook, but his momentum drove him through the punch. He pinned her against the wall with his forearm. Using all his weight to hold her still, he pushed his face up to hers.

'At the airport,' he said. 'It was you, wasn't it?'

Abri struggled and writhed, but Jake pressed his arm up into her throat. The blood rushed to her face. 'I don't know what you're talking about,' she said, her voice a slick, struggling gasp.

She tried to knee him in the groin, but he turned sideways and pressed closer.

'You attacked my mother,' said Jake. 'Tried to steal her camera.'

'So what if I broke her lousy camera?' said Abri.

Jake was stunned. None of this made any sense . . .

Abri bent her knees and stabbed a vicious elbow into Jake's ribs. He doubled up in pain, and she swept his legs away from underneath him. She was on top of him before he could catch his breath. Then she reached back to her ankle and there was something cold at his throat.

A knife.

'Don't even breathe, murderer,' she said.

The blade pressed tight against his neck. The look in her eyes, fierce and full of fire, told Jake that Abri wouldn't hesitate to cut his carotid artery. He'd bleed out on the stairs in less than a minute.

'I didn't kill Sienna,' gasped Jake. 'I came here to make sure you were all right. Y'know, after what happened at the church and the ground. Think about it. I helped you there, didn't I? Why would I do that if I was a killer?'

The pressure on the blade reduced a little, but it was still only a centimetre away from ending his life.

'Abri, I found her like that,' he said. 'Someone came here just before me – she was still warm.'

The flames in her eyes were quenched as tears misted over. Abri climbed off him, sinking back against the stairs. She dropped the knife with a clatter and placed her head in her hands, her shoulders shaking. Jake crouched beside her, and put an arm round her back.

'I'm sorry, Jake,' she said. 'I just saw Sienna . . . like that and you with the club . . .'

'That's OK,' he said. 'Why did you go after me like that? Why did you attack me and my mum at the airport?'

She wiped the tears away. 'I can't explain.'

'Why not? Abri, what are you mixed up in? Is someone after you?'

She didn't say anything.

'You need to trust me,' said Jake. 'Whoever got Sienna may come back for you and Monique.'

A whip-crack sounded in Jake's ear and he caught a shower of sparks on the side of his face.

Abri pushed him down. 'Gun!' she cried.

15

Another round of shots clipped the hand rail and pinged away.

Hurried steps were coming from below. Jake risked peering over the banister. Two floors down, the man in sunglasses with the buzz-cut was pointing the barrel of a gun straight at him. Jake ducked back as another bullet scorched the air.

'Come on!' he shouted to Abri, who was snatching her knife from the floor.

He grabbed the model's hand and pulled her up the stairs after him.

Despite being tired and bruised from their fight, fear drove Jake on. Without a proper weapon, they had no chance against the gunman. Abri kept pace with him as they climbed the stairs. Feet pounded up behind them.

They rounded the landing on the seventh floor. A short

set of steps led to a fire door. Jake smashed into the metal emergency bar and they were on the roof. The rooftop was on two levels. Exits from the other stairwells were placed at regular intervals roughly thirty metres apart, and there were vents dotted around from the air-con units. The hot sun bounced off baked tarmac.

'Over there!' said Abri.

She pointed to the top of a metal fire escape leading off the roof. Jake sprinted after her, but he knew they didn't have enough time to make it.

He heard the door slam open. Jake dragged Abri behind the nearest air-con vent, a chrome flue bent over to stop the rain trickling in. They stood close to each other, as the warm exhaust fumes blasted over them.

Jake peered round the edge of the chimney. The hit man was looking over the fire escape, his gun ready. He turned around slowly, eyeballing the roof. Jake ducked back behind Abri.

'He knows we're up here,' he whispered. 'We've got to create some sort of distraction.' He looked out again. The gunman was doing a circuit of the emergency-exit tower, gun steadied in both hands. Jake saw he was breathing heavily from the climb.

'We're sitting ducks,' hissed Abri.

Jake bent down and picked up a handful of gravel. He threw it in a high arc. The pieces rained down six metres away. The gunman heard and darted over to the source of the sound. Jake gripped Abri's hand again, and led her in the opposite direction.

The gunman turned, levelled and fired. The shot ricocheted off the topside of the vent, and Jake pulled Abri back under cover. He heard a loud rip of clothing. Her top was torn, and a piece hung off the metal.

We're screwed.

'Come out!' said a growling voice. 'I promise I'll make it quick.'

Jake looked into Abri's wide eyes. He shook his head.

'Come and get us!' he shouted.

The hit man's feet crunched closer in the gravel. Jake didn't have a plan. But Abri did. She pulled out her knife again. It didn't look much but it was their only shot.

'Make him come to you,' Abri whispered.

'The other girl didn't suffer much,' said the hit man. 'Neither will you.'

Jake thought about Sienna's bloated, throttled face. She'd suffered, all right. And this guy had probably enjoyed it.

Abri pointed to his side of the vent, and edged the other way.

I get it, he thought. *I keep him busy, and Abri takes him out from the blindside.*

He stuck out his head a fraction.

The hit man was ten metres away. His gun pointed towards the floor.

'That's right. No need to make this messy. Get your hands up.'

Jake stepped out, hands over his head.

'Where's your friend?' asked the shooter.

His head twitched to one side suddenly, and he started to bring the gun round. Something flashed in the air, and the hit man jerked back with a cry, dropping his gun and holding his arm. Abri's knife was buried up to the hilt in his bicep.

He seemed to dance on the spot for a second, then reached up and yanked the knife out. A thick slop of blood spattered the asphalt.

'You freak!' he shouted. 'You're going to pay for that in pain!'

As he reached for the gun, Jake charged. He saw the knife come up and slapped it away. At the same time, Abri came flying in, driving her foot into the hit man's hip. He crumpled to one knee and his gun skittered away.

The hit man stumbled back and Jake went after him, throwing a jab into his nose, and followed up with a cross aimed at the jaw while he was blinking blindly. Somehow, the guy saw enough to turn and deflect the shot with an arm, pulling Jake down on to his knee. Jake's breath went out of him as another blow thudded into the back of his neck and sent him to the ground. He rolled over to see Abri turning through the air, and bringing her foot down in the long arc of a spinning roundhouse. The move would have knocked the hit man out if it had connected properly, but it glanced off his shoulder.

Jake was on his knees and could hardly suck in a breath. Abri was sending punches and low kicks at the gunman, but he was just as quick, keeping his guard tight and blocking hard. Each time she hit his injured arm, blood sprayed from the knife wound. Sienna's killer open-cuffed Abri round the ear, sending her stumbling towards the edge of the building. Jake struggled up, feeling his stomach tighten.

The gunman didn't see him come in. Jake drove a fist into his kidneys. The man dipped in pain, flailing to protect himself. Abri had backed up, but now she stepped in, delivering a side-kick, powerful as a mule, into the hit man's midriff. He staggered towards the building's precipice.

Jake instinctively reached out to grab him, but it was too late. The assassin toppled for half a second on the ledge, arms wheeling, then disappeared over the side. His cry of terror was swallowed by the drop.

Jake and Abri rushed to the edge and looked down. Below, the hit man slammed into a red, green and white café awning, and bounced over the side. He hit an empty table, scattering cutlery and smashing a couple of bottles on the pavement.

From somewhere inside there was a scream.

'Is he dead?' gasped Abri.

Jake shook his head in disbelief. The hit man writhed around for a moment, then slowly climbed to his feet. He stumbled to one side, as though dizzy, then steadied himself against a car.

The hit man looked up, and for a moment their eyes locked.

Then their attacker began walking off quickly down the street.

'Damn it!' said Abri, stamping back across the roof to collect her knife. 'We let him get away!'

'Hey,' said Jake. 'Are you kidding? We nearly got executed out here! We're lucky to be alive!'

Abri picked up the gun too, and popped the clip expertly. She checked the rounds.

'We should have killed him,' she said, reloading and drawing back the barrel. 'For Sienna.'

Jake watched in amazement. One dead body a day was

plenty for him. 'You seemed to know how to handle that . . .'

'We need to get out of here,' she said. 'He might be back.'

'You think so?' said Jake, looking back at the seven-storey drop.

'I'm not taking any chances,' said Abri. 'He probably has friends too.'

She tucked the gun in the back of her jeans and set off along the rooftop.

Jake ran after her, thinking how he'd misjudged Abri Kuertzen by about a mile.

They jumped down on to the lower level, past a nest of antennae and dishes. Abri sped up, and Jake saw why. They were coming to a gap.

'Wait!' he shouted.

But Abri leapt off the edge of the building and landed gracefully on the other side, barely breaking stride. Jake skidded to a halt.

Definitely not your average supermodel.

The leap was only about three metres, but looking down into the narrow alley about twenty metres below, it seemed bigger. Jake walked back to take a run-up, aware of Abri watching him from the other side.

Just pretend it's the long jump at school, he said to himself.

Long drop, more like!

He pelted towards the edge and jumped. It felt like his stomach was trying to escape through his larynx, but he made it, crashing down on the other side, and falling into a roll. As he righted himself, Abri gave him a slap on the back. 'Not bad . . . for a beginner.'

They crossed a couple more flat rooftops until they came to a metal fire escape on the side of a building. There was no way anyone could have tracked them here.

'Ladies first,' Jake said.

Abri climbed down the short ladder and hopped on to the metal grille platform. Jake shot a last glance in the direction from which they'd come, but there was no sign of the hit man on their heels. He went after Abri.

They were halfway down, and Jake was breathing normally again, when he grabbed her arm.

'Wait,' he said. 'You've got some explaining to do.'

'Take your hand off my arm,' she said.

Jake complied, but he wasn't going to let the matter drop. 'You owe me an explanation.'

'How d'you figure that?'

'If this involves my mother, it involves me.'

Abri looked ready to argue for a second, but then relaxed. She brushed her hair away from her face and gave Jake a small nod.

'We never meant for her to be mixed up in it. But she's working for Granble, so . . .'

'What's that supposed to mean?' said Jake. '*You* work for Granble!'

'Only on paper,' said Abri. 'You remember what I said to you back in the church? About his mining group?'

Jake nodded, remembering that same group being mentioned by his father, but kept his mouth shut. There was no need to let on how much he knew − not just yet.

'So many lives have been messed up because of that megalomaniac's actions,' Abri went on. 'Kids working in the mines before they can read, inhumane conditions, terrible accidents. It's economic slavery. Arms dealing too. Granble will shake hands with anyone as long as it makes him richer. Some of us decided to do something about it.'

'You're with the protestors?' said Jake.

'We have similar aims,' said Abri. 'But we like to do things a little . . . *bigger.*'

'Who's we?'

Abri shook her head. 'I shouldn't be telling you any of this.'

'But you are,' said Jake. 'And it sounds like you need as many friends as you can get. Is it just you, Sienna and Monique?'

Abri's lip began to tremble. She nodded. 'Just Monique and me now. We made a pact to bring Granble down.'

And he's not going down lightly, Jake thought.

But there was a piece of the puzzle still missing.

'How does my mum fit into all this? She's not responsible for the mining. She's just another of Granble's employees.'

'She *was*,' said Abri, 'but now she has incriminating evidence against us. A photograph.'

Jake remembered the pictures on the computer. 'Those photos of you on the street . . . they're not just "candid modelling shots", are they?'

'It's complicated,' said Abri. 'She took hundreds of pictures, all around the city. We think she may have unknowingly photographed a . . . *meeting* . . . a face that can't be linked to us.'

'Who?' Jake asked.

'His name's Ferrara. He's a diamond fence. He clears stolen stones on to the market for a cut of the profits.'

The guy on the motorbike, talking to Sienna. It had to be. But why would Sienna be talking to a diamond fence?

As soon as Jake thought it, the answer came to him.

'*You* stole Granble's diamonds.'

16

A bri nodded, a grim smile on her lips.

'But . . . I don't understand . . . You –'

'We rigged the gas canisters on our first visit to the church,' Abri explained. 'Once they went off, we took down the guards posted outside. Monique stood guard while Sienna and I went in with the masks on and did what we had to do.'

She leapt off the bottom of the fire escape and continued walking up the street. Jake could see the outline of the gun under her top. He kicked himself for not working it out it sooner. The thieves – at the airport and in the church – had been so graceful and agile. He'd only thought they were men because they were both tall.

Did I learn nothing from Helga, the ruthless Russian assassin?

'Wait a minute!' he called after her, realising something. 'My *mother* was in that church. I was in there!'

Abri looked back for a moment. 'We would never have hurt anyone . . . well, except Granble and his thugs.'

That didn't seem to be the point, but perhaps this wasn't the time to argue.

'So what now?' he asked, catching up. 'You sell the diamonds and make a big profit? If Granble's operation is as big as you say, won't he just get more diamonds?'

Abri shook her head. They'd reached a corner and she was peering out into the street beyond. 'A man like Granble needs investors to fund the mining work. He's promised them all big returns. Our only chance of bringing him down is to make sure he can't deliver on his promises.'

'And if investment dries up,' said Jake, 'so does the Granble Mining Corporation.'

'Bingo,' said Abri. 'We want to humiliate Granble so much that no one wants to do business with him again. Come on, we have to keep moving.' She broke into a jog across the street.

Jake followed. 'There's got to be a better way,' he said. 'Couldn't you just organise more political opposition? Lobby the South African government?'

Abri snorted as she paused outside a coffee bar. 'Granble's rich enough to buy politicians. Anyway, you've seen how ineffective protesting is. All those placards, all that chanting – it gets nowhere.'

Her chin was slightly raised, challenging him to defy her. Jake could understand her passion, but he still wasn't sure he agreed with her methods. And now that Sienna was dead, what was her next step?

They crossed a car park, and Jake kept his eyes open for Buzz-cut or anyone else who looked threatening. There was a man in builder's overalls leaning against a lamppost, but he seemed more interested in Abri's figure than anything else.

'Do you think Granble's capable of murder?' asked Jake.

'Hundreds die or get injured every year in his mines,' said Abri. 'He's not the sort of guy who gets his own hands dirty, though.'

'Then we should go to the police,' he said.

'No way,' said Abri.

'But until Granble gets his diamonds back you're in danger. So is Monique. He knows it was you who stole his diamonds.'

'We all knew what we were signing up for. Even Sienna.'

Christ, she was *tough*.

'But not me,' said Jake. 'And not my mother.'

Across the street was a police car with the door open and the officer behind the wheel making notes on a pad. Jake started walking over, but Abri grabbed his shoulder. 'Please, Jake. Don't do this.'

Jake paused. *Observe and report*, that's what his dad

140

had said. He probably didn't think that included concealing a murder, abetting a jewel thief, getting shot at and helping a hired hit man in his fall off a building. But MI6 were interested in Granble too. They were coming at him from a different angle, but they were all on the same side, weren't they? And certainly his dad wouldn't want the police sniffing around Granble. Even if the police believed his story – which would probably sound ridiculous to anyone who wasn't involved in it.

'Where are the diamonds now?' said Jake. 'Are they in the flat?'

Abri tensed. 'It's better if you don't know,' she said.

Jake pulled his arm free. The policeman still hadn't noticed them.

'You want me to trust you,' he said. 'Try trusting *me*.'

'I'm trying to keep you *safe*,' she said.

'I don't need you to,' said Jake.

Abri rubbed a hand across her forehead. 'Look, Jake, I need to go and find Monique. She's in danger.'

'Where is she?' asked Jake.

'I don't know,' said Abri. 'The plan was that we all take our diamonds to separate fences, to make sure Granble can't trace them all together. Monique was meeting hers first.'

'And you know where this guy is?' said Jake.

'No,' said Abri. 'We kept that information to ourselves, in case one of us was caught.'

The police officer closed his door and started his engine.

'You think Granble might be tailing her?'

'It's possible.'

Abri took out her phone and speed-dialled a number. Jake watched worry creep over her face as she held it to her ear.

'Damn it! It's the answerphone,' she said. 'Hey, Mon, it's Abs. Listen, something's gone wrong.' She paused, and Jake could see she was weighing up whether to mention Sienna. 'We need to meet. In the square in front of the Duomo. Noon.'

She hung up. 'I really hope she's OK.'

'Why the Duomo?' Jake asked. 'Anyone can see you there.'

'Exactly,' said Abri. 'It's the most open space in the city. Granble would have to be crazy, or desperate, to try something there.'

Jake didn't say that from what he'd seen Granble *was* crazy. And probably desperate too.

He offered a hand to Abri as the police car drove off. 'There's no way you're going there on your own.'

The taxi pulled up at 11.55.

The Duomo rose high above the surrounding buildings, the colour of sand. Its spires and arches reminded Jake of his time in Paris, studying at the Lycée near Notre-Dame. Abri was right. The square was teeming with tourists who consulted guidebooks and posed for photos. There were at least two guided tours making their way to the front of the cathedral. Jake caught snatches from a French group, learning that the Duomo was started in 1386 and was the fourth-largest cathedral in the world.

If he survived today, he had a feeling he would always remember those two bits of trivia.

The tour group drifted away. It looked like such a normal day in the city that Jake found it hard to get a grip on what was happening . . . Sienna's body was, right now, lying dead and cold in a ransacked flat less than a mile away.

From the grim look on Abri's face as she paid the taxi driver, Jake guessed she was thinking similar thoughts.

Jake and Abri tried to blend in. Abri was wearing an Inter Milan cap and a pair of oversize shades bought from a street stall a couple of blocks down from the cathedral. The last thing she wanted was for one of her fans to spot her and cause a scene.

Jake scanned the crowd, looking for Monique. He felt a prickle of nerves in his gut when he couldn't see her.

'We'll wait by the statue,' said Abri, pointing to a sculpture at the edge of the square – a horseman on a pedestal.

Jake kept his eyes peeled as they walked over. If Granble had tracked them here, would it really be that hard for another assassin to blend in with the crowd? He pushed the words 'gun' and 'silencer' out of his mind.

At one minute before noon, a scooter rode up alongside them. Monique flipped back her visor, and kicked out the stand.

'I've got news for you,' she said. 'Something big.' Monique then seemed to notice Jake. 'Hey! What the hell's he doing here?' she said. 'Where's Sienna?'

Abri stepped forwards and placed her hand on Monique's. 'Listen, Mon. Granble's on to us. He killed Sienna.'

Monique sat back in her seat. For a moment, Jake thought she might faint.

'What?' she gasped. 'No!'

'It's true,' said Jake. 'He nearly got Abri too.'

'I don't understand,' choked Monique. 'We were so careful. How could Granble find out? Someone must have told him,' she said, looking at Jake.

'Have you met your fence?' said Abri. 'Have you handed over the diamonds?'

'I'm not saying anything in front of him,' said Monique, jutting her chin out.

Abri slid an arm round her friend. 'Jake's on our side.'

'We don't need allies,' said Monique, clenching her fists. 'Christ, what were you thinking, Abs?' She took off her helmet and ran her hands through her hair. A couple of guys sitting at a table in a café looked over, suddenly interested.

'If you haven't got rid of your diamonds yet, you need to do it ASAP,' Abri said. 'I'll offload mine too. We need to disappear until all this blows over.'

'It's not that simple any more,' said Monique. 'My fence, he told me that the diamonds are —'

Monique seemed to jump a little, then rolled back on her heels. She clutched her chest as though she'd realised she'd left something out of her pocket.

'Mon?' said Abri. 'What's up?'

A trickle of blood escaped from the corner of her mouth. She dropped her hands. They too were covered in blood, and a dark pattern blossomed through her blue jumper.

Jake looked up, sweeping the buildings on all sides. He hadn't even heard the shot.

Sniper!

'. . . they're . . . f-fake,' Monique stammered.

17

'*M**on!*' Abri shrieked.

Jake pulled her away and dived under the nearest table. There was a thump, and a dent appeared in the thick plastic above his head. A bullet. One of the men at the next table shouted '*Mafiosi!*' and people scattered off their chairs in all directions.

'Mon?' said Abri, reaching a hand towards Monique.

'Keep down,' Jake hissed.

Monique toppled sideways on to the ground, dead already. The scooter crashed on top of her legs. A tourist with a camera saw the body and screamed. Others joined the commotion, as blood began to pool under Monique. Abri was frozen beside Jake.

Jake pushed Abri under a sunshade. The shots seemed to have stopped, and with all the gathered people Jake guessed the gunman wouldn't try again.

'We have to leave now,' he said, pulling Abri with him back towards Monique.

At the dead model's side, he gently unhooked her handbag from her arm. A woman shouted something in what Jake thought was German. He ignored her. If there was no ID it would take the police longer to link the killing to Abri and Sienna. Someone else called out in Italian that someone should stop him. Jake saw angry, confused faces gathered around. It wouldn't be long before this crowd turned ugly. He grabbed the bike's handles and pulled it upright.

Abri crouched at Monique's side.

'Get on!' Jake shouted.

Abri suddenly lost her tough veneer. She looked like a lost child. 'I can't,' she said. 'Monique . . .'

'She's gone,' said Jake, tugging her arm. Abri offered little resistance, and climbed up behind him on the scooter. Jake heard the wail of police sirens, not far off. The crowd was thickening, and one of the men from the table in the café came forwards and put his hands on the handlebars.

'Stop!' he said.

I don't have time for this, Jake thought. Abri was holding his waist limply, but not saying anything.

He kicked up the stand, and shoved the Italian roughly in the chest. The guy stumbled over a fallen chair and landed on his backside. He shouted something that Jake could guess wasn't pretty.

'Hold on!' he said to Abri.

Jake gunned the throttle, and the scooter roared off across the square.

A woman leading a toddler pulled her child away, but Jake had already swerved around them. He braked hard as he came to a queue lining up outside the cathedral's main entrance. Looking back, he saw the crowd around Monique was bigger than before. Among them was a police officer wearing a peaked cap. The man whom Jake had shoved to the ground was pointing wildly in their direction.

It wouldn't be long.

Jake yanked the handlebars around. He saw the police officer walking swiftly across the square towards him. Abri's grip tightened round his middle.

'That way!' she said, finding her voice again. She pointed to a road leading off the side of the square. Via Ugo Foscolo.

The police officer shouted, and his hat fell off his head as he broke into a run. Jake twisted the throttle, jinked around a street-sweeper and into traffic. A barrage of horns announced the drivers' displeasure. Jake ignored them, cutting across two lanes of traffic and into the small side road. Shops selling postcards and tourist paraphernalia lined the street and it was busy with people.

Jake mounted the pavement to avoid a black-clad old lady with a small dog, but clipped one of the postcard stands with his outstretched knee. It spun round, and cards cascaded across the street like confetti. Jake heard someone shouting, *'Oh mio Dio!'*

At the other end of the street, two more police appeared. Jake braked and put down his foot. They were trapped.

Or maybe not, thought Jake. On the opposite side of the road, between an ice-cream parlour and a stall selling miniature models of the Duomo, the Leaning Tower of Pisa and the Colosseum, there was what looked like an alleyway. Jake lifted his foot and steered the bike towards it. Sure enough, a narrow passage threaded past dustbins to what looked like an exit about fifty metres down.

'Hang on!' he told Abri. 'And keep your knees tucked in.'

'You can't go down there!' she gasped. 'It's not wide enough.'

Jake tucked the front wheel into the alley. Abri was wrong: there were about two centimetres either side of the handlebars. Not much, but enough.

Jake moved the bike slowly, keeping it steady. Gradually he built up speed. They ripped over a discarded pizza box and other rubbish. At the far end, they hit a main road.

Jake waited for a moment, then he steered back into traffic. There were dozens of other scooters and, in a few seconds, he was confident that they'd be lost in the pack.

'Are they still following us?' he asked Abri, then felt her twist in the seat.

'I don't think so,' she said, 'but keep going.'

Jake took a couple more turns, driving away from the cathedral and into more residential areas. After a few hundred metres, he saw the turning to an underground car park and steered the bike down the ramp.

He didn't realise how hard he was focusing until he killed the engine. Sweat was dripping down his back and his heart was pounding like a jackhammer. Abri climbed off and he did the same. She leant against a concrete column with one hand and bent over, dry-retching.

Jake's mind was racing.

Fake diamonds? That's what Monique had said, wasn't it? He shook his head to clear it.

'We have to get you to the police – you need protection,' he said to Abri.

'This is crazy,' she said, wiping her mouth. 'This can't be happening.'

'It is,' said Jake. 'Someone killed Sienna and Monique, and you're going to be next.'

'But the diamonds . . .' Abri began.

'Forget the diamonds,' said Jake. 'We need to hand them over to the police. It's the only way to stop the killing.'

'But what about me?' asked Abri. 'I'll be arrested.'

Jake didn't say anything. Better that than strangled or bleeding out while tourists took their holiday snaps.

'I can't believe they're both dead,' said Abri, the tears welling in her eyes. 'We were in this together, from the start . . .'

As the first tear trickled down her cheek, she fell against Jake's shoulder. He put his arm round her and kept his eyes on the entrance to the car park. The police were on the lookout for a killer and Jake realised that they were the prime suspects. It would only take one trigger-happy policeman and they'd both be killed.

Abri sniffed and looked up. With her bloodshot eyes and messy hair, it was easy to forget that she was a supermodel.

'I don't want to go to prison,' she said.

Jake tried to think through the options. They couldn't stay on the run forever. Either Granble or the police would catch them. If they gave themselves up willingly, explained the situation with a lawyer present, then perhaps Abri would get off with a lighter sentence.

'If Monique was right, you only stole fake diamonds from Granble,' he said.

'I don't get it,' said Abri. 'She must have been wrong.'

'Those were her last words,' said Jake.

'But why would Granble use fakes?' asked Abri. 'He's all about the flawless quality of his stones. His guy had a briefcase handcuffed to his wrist. That's serious precautions for a bunch of phoney stones.'

Jake remembered Granble's terrier preventing his mum taking close-ups. It made sense – fake diamonds would not have stood up to the close scrutiny of a camera lens.

'Maybe for appearance's sake,' said Jake. 'I mean, the crown jewels in the Tower of London are all replicas. Granble clearly *wants* people to believe the stones are the real deal.'

'But the shoot was top secret – there was so much security. Why go to such lengths? If the protection's there, he could just use the real stones.'

Jake shrugged. 'Well, your little stunt proved that wasn't the case, right?'

Abri nodded. 'We need to get to the bottom of this. For Sienna and Monique.'

A new plan was forming in the back of Jake's mind. The police couldn't be trusted to bring the models' killers to justice, and Jake would bet his last euro that Granble would distance himself from any connection to the scandal. If the diamonds *were* fake, then his dad needed to know. It could be crucial in his mission to bring down Granble.

'Come on,' he said. 'We need to get away from here.'

'You're not going to turn me in?' Abri said.

'That depends,' Jake replied.

'On what?'

'On whether you can trust me.'

18

Silence descended over the car park.

'Tell me where the diamonds are,' Jake said.

Abri shook her head. 'Me, the girls – we had a pact. I can't.'

'The girls are dead,' said Jake, more harshly than he needed to. 'The pact is void.'

Abri walked towards a far wall of the car park. Her body language said it all – she wanted to be away from this.

'I can help you,' Jake pressed.

'You'll be in danger too, if I tell you.'

'I'm in danger already,' said Jake.

Abri put her hands on her hips and looked towards the ceiling. Her lips moved silently. Jake could see she was coming round, running out of options.

She pursed her lips, and gave him a long stare. 'They're at the church,' she said.

It took Jake a second to process. 'The church where you did the photo shoot?'

'Yeah.'

Jake shook his head in wonder. 'The last place Granble would think to look.'

He made a mental calculation. Half an hour to get to the church, then another twenty minutes to deliver the fake diamonds to his dad.

He sat back on the bike. 'Where are they exactly?' he asked Abri, kicking away the stand.

'Hey!' she said. She advanced towards him. 'You're not going without me!'

'You should stay out of the way,' said Jake. 'I can handle this myself.'

'No way,' said Abri. She planted her feet in front of the bike, and gripped the handlebars. Her hands over his. 'You won't be able to find the diamonds without me.'

Jake thought about the church. It wasn't that big. He could find them on his own.

'I don't have time for this,' said Jake. 'I'm trying to look after you.'

Abri moved away and swung her leg over the saddle behind him. She put her lips close to his ear.

'Then trust *me*,' she said.

Jake twisted the throttle and sent the scooter up the ramp.

They drove back to the church, taking the back roads as often as possible. Abri gave him a nudge when she spotted a police car in the distance, and Jake pulled over beside a monument to Vittorio Emanuele, until it had cruised past. By now he was sure the authorities across the city would have a half-decent description of a young man and beautiful woman whizzing around the city on a blue Vespa. The only thing going in their favour was that in Milan, Vespas were everywhere. And hot women were hardly an endangered species in Italy's fashion capital.

Jake wondered if he should call his dad now. Once Monique's identity hit the airwaves and TV stations, the link with Abri would be made quickly. Jake could see it clearly in his mind's eye. His mum would be on the phone to his dad, or vice versa. There would be shouting. *He was supposed to be with you . . . No, you were looking after him.*

But if Jake called him now he knew exactly what his dad would say. *Forget the diamonds. Come to me.* And hell was going to freeze over before Jake took a step back from this. Abri needed him.

There was no time to lose.

They stopped at some lights, and Jake checked his mirrors. Two cars back was a silver Fiat that he was sure he'd seen pass them at the monument. But they'd made several turns since then. He couldn't make out the driver's face past his sunshade, but there was no one else in the car. He twisted to speak to Abri.

'Just going to take a little detour,' he said. 'Make sure we're not being tailed.'

He indicated right, and saw the Fiat do the same.

Jake's skin prickled.

As soon as the lights went orange, he skidded away with a stink of burnt rubber and gave the bike throttle. He put another fifty yards between them and the Fiat, then took another right, then a left into a courtyard surrounded by office buildings. He turned the bike round and stalled. Abri's grip round his waist tightened.

'You think someone's behind us?' she said.

A couple of seconds later, the silver car cruised slowly past. The driver was looking the other way and didn't see Jake.

'Not any more,' he said.

Twenty minutes later, Jake parked the bike across the square from the church to make sure all was quiet. They waited five minutes, but he only saw an elderly lady carrying a netted bag of tomatoes and courgettes.

They jogged together across the square as the late afternoon sun dipped away behind the buildings opposite. The front gates were bolted from the inside, so they went to the side door where the security guards had been standing. That, too, wouldn't budge.

Jake took a step back, ready to kick, but Abri put an arm across his chest.

'Let me try.'

'Sure,' said Jake. *What? She's going to kick it down?* No way could she kick through a door.

Abri took one of the pins from her hair and dug around in her bag. She fished out a nail file. Crouching by the lock, she inserted both. Her tongue played along her top lip as she concentrated, fiddling the file and pin up and down. The lock gave a soft click.

She didn't learn that *on the catwalk*, thought Jake, impressed.

Inside, the church was gloomy and cold, and no light streamed through the stained glass. All of the lighting equipment and photo-shoot set-up had gone. The only signs that anyone had been here were a few cigarette butts, some discarded wiring and Granble Diamond Company business cards left stranded on the floor.

Jake wondered if whoever was in that suspicious silver

Fiat might have guessed their destination.

'Let's be quick,' he said.

'Follow me.' Abri paced quickly up the central aisle towards the front of the church. When she got to the altar, she stopped and threw off the black cloth that covered it. This was the very scene of the crime. *What's she doing?*

He saw there was a double-door compartment in the back of the altar, which Abri pulled open. She reached inside to a shelf and brought out two velvet bags.

'Monique already took hers,' she said sadly.

She closed the doors and laid out the cloth on top of the altar again, then loosened the drawstrings on the bags and carefully tipped the contents on to the altar.

Jake gasped as the stones seemed to sparkle from a thousand surfaces at once.

'If those are fakes,' he said, 'they're awesome ones.'

'You're telling me,' said Abri, lifting a necklace and placing it against her tanned neck. 'I saw drawings of all the Granble pieces before the shoot, and these are identical to the real thing.'

'Then someone on the inside must have made them.'

A shuffle of footsteps filled the silence of the nave, and Abri's head snapped up.

Jake scanned the shadows. Abri's breathing was heavy

beside him. He pulled her away, behind the lectern.

'Who is it?' she hissed.

Jake put a finger to his lips. Whoever it was, they were in trouble.

He heard the slow click of shoe-heels on the flagged floor of the church, and peered round the edge of the lectern. No one appeared.

Shit. The diamonds were still on top of the altar. Apart from the necklace. He looked at it, dangling from Abri's hand. She seemed to understand, gave a small nod, then dipped it down her top.

Clever, thought Jake. *If we get out of this, that might be the only evidence we have.*

It was a very big 'if'.

19

'You shouldn't have taken what wasn't yours,' said the voice. South African.

Jake peered out again, between the panels of the lectern. At the back of the church was the stocky figure of Granble's right-hand man, Jaap, and he was carrying what looked like a submachine gun, strapped over his shoulder and aimed at the floor.

'The good thing about this place is that it's out of the way,' he said. 'Just a pity that two more kids with such *promising* futures will have to die.'

He hardly sounded sorry.

'No one needs to get hurt,' said Jake. 'Just take the diamonds, and go.'

The footsteps stopped. 'That's not how it works,' Jaap said. 'Mr Granble doesn't want any loose ends.'

'We won't tell anyone,' promised Abri. 'Why would we?

We'd end up in prison for theft.'

Jaap gave a low chuckle. 'Nice try, sweetheart.'

Jake guessed that the South African was still six metres away. Their best chance was to split up, divert his attention. He tapped Abri on the shoulder and pointed back towards the choir stalls. He mouthed 'Go!' Her face creased with uncertainty for a second, so he jabbed his finger back again. This time she listened, and began to back away in a low crouch.

'Why are the diamonds so important to you, anyway?' said Jake. 'We know they're not real.'

He heard a gun click.

'Oh, do we?' said Jaap. 'Even more reason to make sure you don't leave this place alive.'

Jake followed Abri, staying out of Jaap's line of sight.

The South African continued, 'Seems that Mr Granble's mines weren't quite as perfect as he thought. Sure, we got a few promising rocks out, but it was much harder than anticipated.'

'From what I heard,' Jake said, 'if Granble wants more workers, he gets them. There's no shortage of kids.'

'That's not the problem,' said Jaap. 'He's got the workers, he's got the machinery, but the stones aren't there − at least, not the flawless ones the world thinks he's got.'

Jake remembered Granble's angry phone calls during the

shoot, and suddenly got it. 'Ah, so he needs the fakes to get the moneymen on board?'

And by the time they find out the truth Granble's pocketed their cash.

He shuffled into the stalls beside Abri.

'There's no way out of here,' said Jaap. From the sound of his voice and the tinkle of stones, Jake assumed he had reached the altar.

Jake looked about. Granble's chief goon was right. One way in, one way out. He had the remaining diamonds, and soon he and Abri would be dead.

Jake spotted a torn prayer book on the ground. Not much use as a weapon, but maybe as a distraction. He closed his hand round it.

'I'm bored,' said Jaap. 'If you come out now, I promise to make it quick.'

Jake whispered to Abri, 'Ready?'

She nodded.

He swung his arm, flinging the book in a high arc into the opposite stall. It landed with a thud. Jaap's steps were quick as he darted between the stalls. Jake peeped over the edge of his and saw Jaap's back to him as he scouted the source of the sound. *Now or never.*

Jake climbed over the stall and threw himself on to

Jaap's back. The South African grunted and fell forwards against the railing of the stall, but managed to stay upright. A rat-a-tat of bullets sprayed aimlessly from the gun, churning splinters out of the wood. Jake yanked back, taking Jaap with him. They collapsed on the ground. Jake pushed the gun aside with his left hand, and gave Jaap a flurry of punches and elbows to the face, bloodying his fist.

He thought he had him, but Jaap's arm thrashed up and the gun hit the side of Jake's face, sending him into a dizzy sprawl. Jaap was up on one knee, levelling the weapon. Suddenly Abri was there, and she delivered a brutal kick into the base of Jaap's spine with the point of her foot. He screamed in agony and dropped forwards. Her second kick sent the gun spinning away.

Jake struggled up and grabbed her arm. 'Come on!'

They ran the length of the nave back towards the side door, but Jake's heart sank. It was locked again. Jake swung his foot at the door, but it did nothing except jar his knee. He took a few steps back and charged with his shoulder. It rattled in the frame, but didn't break. Then he remembered the side door into the vestry. *Perhaps it was still open now!*

He could hear Jaap groaning in the stalls.

Abri followed as he led the way towards the vestry. As they neared the doorway, something exploded in Jake's ears.

A round of bullets scuffed up white dust from the stone walls two metres away. Jaap was up, and stumbling behind the altar.

Jake yanked Abri into the vestry and went straight over to the small door. With his heart thudding, he gave it a kick. But the door didn't budge. Someone must have boarded it up after the robbery.

'Damn it!' he hissed. He scanned the room quickly. The windows were barred. There was only one other door. In the corner, the one that must lead up into the steeple tower. It wasn't a way out, but it was a place to hide. 'Up there,' he whispered.

Jaap's footsteps slapped on the stone outside the vestry as Jake and Abri ran up a spiral staircase, leaning against the wall for balance. It was only wide enough to go single file, and the narrow stone treads were worn smooth. They passed the mezzanine floor and carried on. At least Jaap would have a hard job following them.

Near the top, Abri slipped and he dragged her to her feet. They climbed the final few steps, and found themselves in a small square space with a wooden balustrade surrounding a huge, green-stained metal bell. There were slits in the thick stone walls, but they weren't wide enough to climb through. Even if they could, the drop was fifteen metres. Jake kicked through the balustrade, and snapped off one of the spindle railings. Splinters showered below. Now he had some sort of weapon at least.

He looked back down the steps, trying to control his panting. After half a minute, a shadow of a man with a gun appeared against the wall. Jake bristled. If they charged Jaap in the tiny stairwell, he wouldn't be able to get many bullets off.

Perhaps Abri can escape.

He looked back at her. 'I'm going to face up to him,' he said, brandishing the piece of wood. 'I'll distract him, then you get past.'

'*Distract* him?' said Abri. 'He'll kill you!'

'If we wait up here,' said Jake, 'we're sitting ducks again.'

The shadow disappeared from below. The stairwell was silent. They waited.

Where'd he go? Jake wondered.

'Listen,' said Abri, 'we need another plan. I'm not going to let you –'

Jake put up his hand as a smell tickled his nostrils. Smoke. At first he wondered whether it was coming from outside. But then he saw the faint spiral of smoke coming up the steps. There was enough wood in the stairwell for it to catch quickly.

He took a few steps down, and saw a flickering orange glow. The sound of crackling grew louder, and the smoke thicker. He pulled up his T-shirt over his mouth and coughed, and went down further. Suddenly a staccato burst of bullets ripped across the wall near his head, ricocheting up off the steps. Jake ducked back.

'You've got two choices,' shouted Jaap. 'Come down here and face me, or stay up there and choke to death. Either way it's time to say your prayers.'

Jake ran back up the stairs in the dense smoke and found Abri pressed against the outer wall of the bell tower, trying to suck air through one of the gaps. She broke off spluttering.

Jake pushed her down to the ground where the air was clearer, but he could hardly breathe. 'He's trying to smoke us out,' he said.

'Then we're trapped,' said Abri.

Below, he could hear the fire raging in the church. Jake wiped the tears out of his burning eyes. He saw the bell. *There's another way*.

'Abri,' Jake coughed. 'Stay here, I'm going down.'

'What are you going to do?'

Jake pointed to the bell mechanism, with the rope hanging off. 'I'm going that way.'

Abri's face was smeared with dirt. 'You're crazy!'

'Any better ideas? You have about five seconds to share them.'

Abri's body shook with a coughing fit. 'Good luck, Jake.'

He stood up and looked down the rope shaft. About a metre across, he guessed. It was too risky to use the rope itself – the bell would start clanging and let Jaap know he was coming. But he could climb down by lodging his feet and hands against the side. He'd done a bit of rock climbing in France; they called this 'chimneying'. Jake sat on the edge, and supported himself with his hands as he reached across with his legs. The air was fairly clear in the tower. But it looked a long way down.

Jake let his body weight tip over the edge, and made sure his grip was firm on either side. Then he started shifting downwards, a few centimetres at a time. Soon he had a rhythm going. His arms ached, but he'd covered seven metres without trouble. About ten more to go. He didn't know what he'd find at the bottom, but hopefully Jaap would be looking the other way, guarding the base of the stairwell.

Then the wall seemed to crumble and his foot shot away. For a split second, Jake was falling. He flapped with his arms and his fingers found the rope. His grip tightened and the strands burnt into his palms. He cried out in pain and found himself swinging back and forth, smashing into the sides of the tower.

Sound boomed around him.

The bell!

He looked down. If Jaap had heard, he'd . . .

The assassin stepped out below the bell tower, looking up.

His eyes met Jake's and he fumbled for his gun.

20

J ake let go of the rope and dropped like a stone. He
slammed into Jaap feet first before he could get a
shot off. They crumpled in a heap, and pain shot through
Jake's thigh.

Jake rolled off, and tried to stand. His leg wouldn't work.
Jaap lay completely still on his front. Wood was stacked up at
the bottom of the stairwell, with fragments of tapestries and
drapes driving the flames. There was no way up or down using
the stairs. All one side of the church was ablaze, with flames
licking up the walls into the wooden rafters above. Thick
clouds of black smoke poured across the floor and heat came
over Jake in waves. He sucked in a hot breath and limped to
the bottom of the rope.

'Abri!' he shouted. He waited. The smoke was so thick now,
and filling the tower too. He couldn't even see the bell above.
'Climb down!' he yelled. 'It's safe!'

No sound. Jake felt desperation grip his insides. Had she already passed out from the smoke?

The rope twitched and a pale leg appeared through the smoke. Jake's heart leapt. Abri shimmied down speedily, hand over hand, like she'd done this a hundred times.

She probably had.

She dropped the last two metres, and Jake caught her. 'You did it!' he said.

'*You* did it,' she smiled, nodding to Jaap's inert body. 'Has he got the key?'

Jake bent down painfully on one knee and rifled through Jaap's pockets. He found the key. As he stood up, the whole building seemed to rumble as though shaken by an earthquake. Something cracked above, and Jake saw one of the roof beams shift. He dived into Abri, and pulled her away as a shower of smoking debris came down. Part of the roof had collapsed and Jake could see the dusk sky through the hole. But, worst of all, the only unlocked door was completely blocked off by tonnes of fallen masonry and glowing embers.

The vestry door was boarded up, Jaap had locked the side gate again and the big front doors didn't seem to have been opened in years. There might be a key somewhere, but he didn't have time to look for it. There was no other way out. All the windows were barred.

Except one. Jake saw the huge stained glass window at the far end of the church behind the choir stalls. Its base was a good two and a half metres off the ground, but if they pushed a chair up they'd be able to jump.

He pulled Abri with him, sticking close to the walls in case any more of the roof collapsed. His leg complained with every step, and his throat felt like he'd swallowed hot coals. The smoke hung in clouds like thick drapes. He could barely see two metres ahead.

Abri was gasping into her elbow, but Jake didn't let go of her hand. Back through the choir stalls, they reached the end of the church. With Abri's help, Jake pushed a pew underneath the window. He stepped back and picked up a chair, hoisting it over his head. With a cry from the bottom of his parched lungs he launched it at the decorative window.

Glass exploded out, then fell away in glittering shards. There were a few jagged areas left. Jake ripped off his shirt, scattering buttons. He tore it into rough strips and handed two to Abri.

'You go first!' he said. 'Wrap your hands.'

She did as he said and climbed on to the pew. Jake got up beside her. He offered his hands to give her a foot-up on to the ledge, and she scrambled over. Jake lost his balance and fell back on to the floor. His eyes stung and he felt like he suddenly weighed a tonne. He told his legs to climb up again, and they did, but so slowly it was like wading through mud. He jumped up and felt for the ledge with his fingers, but he didn't have the strength to pull himself up.

The fire against his back was like the worst sunburn he could imagine, spreading over his skin. He felt his fingers slipping off the ledge, the tendons in his arms burning.

I can't make it, he thought. *I've got nothing left.*

Then fingers gripped his wrists. Jake managed to look up. Abri's lips were moving wildly. She was shouting.

'Come on, Jake! Don't give up.'

He found a last reserve of strength, and pulled. He felt the ledge across his stomach, fresh air on his face. He toppled over the edge, and his feet swung over with him. The ground came up fast, and he fell happily on to it.

He must have passed out for a couple of seconds, because he came to on his front, his mouth thick with the taste of burnt wood. Jake rolled over and saw that Abri was lying on her back. She wasn't moving.

'Abri!' Jake said, crawling over.

Relief flooded him as she moved her arm weakly. Spluttering coughs made her body spasm. Jake came to her side – his hands were bleeding where he'd climbed out of the window, and his eyes were burning. He put a hand on Abri's shoulder and knee and rolled her into the recovery position.

'You'll breathe better like that,' he said.

Smoke poured out of the broken window; the fire raged with the sound of cracking twigs. Even out here, the heat prickled over Jake's face. The church was like a furnace. Jake was sure of one thing: Jaap wouldn't be coming out alive.

It wouldn't be long before the fire brigade were on the scene. Jake sucked in more clean air – he and Abri had to move, *now*.

Suddenly there was a screech of brakes.

Jake looked back and saw two black estates had pulled up. Three doors popped open and three guys in tracksuits jumped out. They didn't look friendly. From the other car a man in a suit looked through an open window, while speaking on the phone. He nodded, then shouted to his henchmen. 'Get the boy and girl.'

It didn't make sense. A Scottish accent?

Jake tried to stand, but his legs wobbled beneath him. He fell back, weak and dizzy. One guy, muscles bulging through his shirt, went straight to Abri and heaved her up.

'Get off her!' shouted Jake, trying to swing his foot at the kidnapper's legs.

Firm hands gripped his armpits, then twisted his arm behind his back.

'You're coming with us,' said an English accent. 'There's no time to argue.'

Jake tried to wrench free, but they weren't letting go.

Two guys pushed him towards the cars. The boot was open, and Abri was laid inside with ease by the heavily-muscled guy.

There's no way I'm going in there, thought Jake. Granble was probably going to have them driven to a quiet place outside the city so that he could finish what Jaap had started. He pushed with his heels against the gravel, but his legs were hoisted off the ground and before he could fight, he too was in the boot beside Abri. He writhed into a more comfortable position in the confined space, but still her hair was in his face, choking him.

Jake tried to turn over, and saw the three guys looking down, the smoke-filled sky behind them. 'Feet in if you wanna keep them,' said the English one.

Jake tucked his legs up. The guy slammed the boot, and the rectangle of daylight disappeared. Everything was black.

The doors slammed in quick bursts, then the engine turned over and rumbled into life. The sounds seemed magnified in the enclosed space. Jake was disorientated. He couldn't tell where they were headed. At one point after setting off, he heard sirens and imagined it must be the fire-fighters heading to the ruined church.

'Jake . . .' Abri said.

'I'm here,' Jake replied. He tried to shift his cramped body to give her more room. This was up close and personal, but not how he'd imagined.

'Who are those people?' Abri said. 'Granble's men?'

'I guess so,' said Jake. He lifted his head, his eyes adjusting to the darkness. Perhaps he could open the boot from the inside. Jump out when they slowed at lights. He felt for a release catch, but there was nothing. There wasn't room to get a good strong kick in, not that either of his legs would respond. All he could do was be ready and waiting when they stopped. But would he even get a chance? These guys had killed before.

The only thing we'll get when that boot opens is a bullet to the head.

21

Occasionally Jake heard other traffic nearby, and the blast of horns. That was a good sign.

We're not leaving the city.

He managed to roll on to his front and ball up into a low crouch. At least when that boot did open, he'd be ready.

They drove for about twenty minutes by Jake's guess, before the car slowed.

'Don't make a move until I do,' he said to Abri. 'Let me take the lead.'

If bullets were going to fly, they stood more chance if they worked together.

The car slowed to a stop and the driver killed the engine. Abri's breath was coming in rapid pants now.

The doors cracked open, slow and menacing. Jake's heart was hammering through his ribs. He clenched his fists, tensed his legs to spring. 'Let them out,' said a low voice.

The boot catch clicked. Jake pushed up with all his strength and the hatch flew open. He saw Mr Muscles and swung his fist. It connected clean on the point of his chin and Jake toppled forwards, making sure his momentum caused him to fall on to the guy, who cried out in surprise.

Jake rolled up off the floor, waiting for the next attack, his eyes scanning for a gun. No one pounced. The other guys were standing well back in a circle. And none were armed. Slowly, the scene came into focus. They were in an underground car park. The man on the floor was on his haunches, rubbing his chin and flexing his jaw.

'God, Steve . . . your boy packs a good one.'

Steve?

Jake spun round and saw his dad with his arms folded across his chest. He was wearing a dark suit and grey tie. And, unless Jake was mistaken, some discreet make-up. The sound of distant cheering reached his ears. It was a noise Jake would recognise anywhere. They were in a football stadium.

The San Siro . . .

'It was his mother who insisted on the boxing lessons,' his dad said to his friend, who was getting up off the floor.

Jake lowered his fists. 'What's going on?'

Abri was climbing tentatively out of the boot and Jake couldn't help thinking that she still looked like a model.

The black smudges on her face, the tangled hair and the torn clothing could have been staged for a shoot.

'I might ask you the same question,' his dad replied. He looked gravely at Abri. 'Monique Herne and Sienna Coppola are both dead.'

Abri gave a defiant nod. 'We know.'

If that surprised his dad, he didn't show it.

'We heard the police were tracking two teenagers, a guy and a girl, on Herne's Vespa. We only managed to track you down by triangulating your phone, Jake. If we hadn't –'

'I can explain –' Jake started.

His dad interrupted. 'What part of observe and report did you not understand?'

Jake started to protest.

His dad raised an eyebrow, then looked at his watch. 'Well, we have about twenty-five minutes before kick-off.'

The other men disappeared into their cars, and his dad led Jake and Abri upstairs, saying he had to be in the commentary box for the start of the game. They got a few odd looks from the various behind-the-scenes runners on the way, but Jake's dad rushed them through. He listened patiently as Jake outlined what had happened since leaving his mum's that morning. More than once he shook his head or pinched the top of his nose in dismay, but he didn't interrupt. Jake wasn't sure what he was allowed to say in front of Abri, but so far his dad hadn't sent her away. He guessed she might be an important source of information for him now about Granble's activities.

Maybe the *only* source.

They washed up as best they could in his dad's dressing room. Luckily Jake could fit into his dad's spare clothes, and he tossed his smoke and blood-stained rags into a bin. Abri charmed another presenter out of his extra shirt and belt, which she wore over her top. In her makeshift dress, she looked ready for the catwalk.

'It's a good job we got to you when we did,' his dad said. 'If the police or fire brigade had found you at the church, you could have jeopardised everything. Jake, what *were* you thinking?'

'Don't blame him,' interrupted Abri. 'He was trying to protect me.'

'Young lady, I know some people who will want to talk to you. Not the police,' he assured her. 'But people who want to bring down Granble as much as you do. This is bigger than your little group can handle, evidently.'

Jake swallowed. *Does he have to be so harsh? She's lost her two best friends.*

Perhaps his dad was thinking the same thing, because he softened his tone.

'I'm glad you're both safe. If what you say about this accomplice of Granble – what was his name, Jaap? – is true, then Granble probably thinks you're both dead. That buys us time. We've asked the police to keep an embargo on announcing the deaths of your colleagues. My ex-wife has arranged for some of the players' wives and girlfriends to take their place.' He paused to check his watch again. 'It's a shame we don't have any proof of these fake diamonds. Our guys won't be able to get near the wreckage of the church –'

'Wait!' said Abri. She reached inside her top. Jake grinned as she pulled out the diamond necklace. She handed it to his father. He held the necklace up and watched it sparkle in the dressing-room lights.

'You're telling me these *aren't* real?'

'Practically worthless,' said Abri.

His dad whistled.

'So we've got him,' said Jake. 'We can take Granble down –'

'Not so fast,' his dad said, holding up a palm. 'This isn't enough. Granble will just deny knowledge of it. Or he'll make it sound like some sort of security arrangement – using fakes in case of theft. Christ, he'll probably turn it into a positive and get even more investors.'

'But we can't let him get away with it,' Jake said. He felt

his blood start to boil.

'I think we'll have to let this one pass,' his dad said. 'The runway show's at half-time. Our sources say that Granble's managed to get diamonds from another source at short notice. My guess is that he's paying through the nose for it, but for appearances' sake it'll keep his investors happy.'

'So Granble walks?' said Abri.

Jake's dad nodded sharply. Jake felt a measure of comfort that it seemed to make his dad as angry as he was. 'For now.'

'Just like Popov,' Jake said quietly. 'The guy's a crook, a murderer, and we watch him walk away with everything.'

'What about Sienna and Monique?' said Abri. 'They didn't give their lives for nothing.'

Jake's dad's face remained impassive. 'I'm sorry. There's nothing more we can do at this time. We'll monitor Granble over the coming months –'

'No way!' said Abri. She marched towards the door and yanked it open, only to find the beefcake who Jake had floored earlier.

'I'm afraid we can't let you jeopardise our intelligence work,' said Jake's dad. 'Frank will keep you here until after the game. For your own safety.'

'You can't do this,' said Abri, squaring up to Frank.

She looked fierce enough, but Frank didn't look impressed.

'Dad!' said Jake, gripping his father's arm. 'She's on our side.'

His dad looked for a second at Jake's hand.

'Listen, Jake. Granble's sitting up in the VIP box at the moment. I doubt he'll even stay around after half-time. He's a clever guy. If we try to take him without enough evidence, he'll make it a hundred times harder for us next time. You must understand that a man like him doesn't just present you with an open goal. He puts eleven men behind the ball and hits you on the break.'

Jake let go of his father's arm. He felt like punching a hole in the wall. 'I get it.'

His dad straightened his collar and sleeves. 'Now I have a game to commentate on in ten minutes.' He raised the tiny roving mic a few inches up his lapel. 'How do I look?'

Jake was still looking at the mic, and a plan was forming in his mind.

'Jake?'

Jake felt a slow smile spreading over his face. 'What if we could get Granble to confess?'

'Enough of this,' said his dad sternly. 'I've got to go.'

'No, wait,' said Jake. 'I know what we need to do. Hear me out.'

His dad checked his watch. 'You have two minutes . . . Convince me.'

Fifty minutes later, Jake stood backstage behind the catwalk. His mum was snapping shots of the WAGs trying to look natural in ridiculous designer dresses. One of the women was practically tangerine orange with fake tan and another was trying to stop her implants busting over the top of her corset dress. Some of Granble's people were draping diamonds over the models.

'Kid, pass me those pins,' said a small Asian-American man. He was the designer whose clothes were being showcased alongside Granble's rocks. He was flustered, running around between various chattering models, making last-minute adjustments to the designer dresses that passed for fashion. Jake held out a pin cushion and the man took two in his mouth and one in each hand. He didn't even say thank you. Another time Jake might have said something, but his mind was only on the half-time whistle.

It had taken all of the two minutes to persuade his dad that his plan could work. It was risky, but if he'd learned one thing about Granble it was that he liked to show off. Jake's scheme rested on that assumption.

'Hey, handsome,' said a sexy Afrikaans accent.

Jake turned to see Abri lighting up the whole backstage

area with a smile. Jake gasped. She was dressed chest to ankle in a pale blue silk dress that flowed over her curves like water. Her shoulders were bare, and her blonde hair fell over them in loose curls. Hard to believe that an hour ago she'd looked like a chimney sweep.

'You'll do,' said the designer, rushing past and giving Abri an appraising up-and-down glance.

'You look amazing,' said Jake.

'Thanks,' said Abri. 'What a little make-up can do for a girl, huh?'

'You sure you want to do this?' said Jake. 'Granble will see you up there.'

'I'll do it for Sienna and Monique,' she said. 'Just make sure you get him for all of us.'

Jake tapped the top pocket of his shirt, where a roving mic had been concealed. He was wearing a flesh-coloured earpiece the size of a sim card in his ear. 'Ready to go.'

Abri smiled. 'Fasten this for me, will you?' She held out the fake diamond necklace.

'Nice touch,' said Jake. He fastened the clasp of the necklace on the back of her neck. The fine hairs lifted slightly as they brushed against his fingers.

When she turned again, she was closer than before. Really close.

'I'm sorry you got mixed up in all this, Jake,' she said.

'It had its advantages,' he said.

Abri grinned, and looked away for a second. Then she raised up on to her tiptoes and pressed her lips against his. It took him by surprise, but he put his arm round her waist and kissed her back. When they parted, there was a slight flush on her cheeks.

'Thank you,' she said. 'For everything.'

A runner came in. 'Five minutes till the half-time whistle,' he shouted. 'Everyone at their stations.'

Abri gave Jake another quick peck on the cheek. 'Good luck, Jake.'

She turned and ran to join the WAGS, who eyed her enviously.

Jake wondered if he'd ever see her again. The Italian police would need to talk to her at some point. She might even be arrested before the game was over.

He left the backstage area and found the elevator that would take him up to the VIP spectator boxes. To Granble.

It's all up to me now.

22

The lift doors opened and Jake stepped inside. He could still feel the electric tingle of Abri's lips on his.

All too soon, the lift stopped and the doors opened.

He showed the backstage pass and marched along the corridor. The spectators roared and the ground vibrated, like a giant beast stirring. Jake knew what that meant. Half-time.

'Can you hear me, Dad?' he said.

There was a tiny crackle of static, then his dad's voice came over the earpiece, faint but clear. 'I got you, Jake. Take it easy. If it looks like he's not playing, abort. You got me?'

'Roger,' said Jake.

'You can call me Dad,' his father said, deadpan. Then added, 'Seriously, be careful, Jake.'

The VIP boxes were marked with the names of whatever corporate group or celebrity had hired them out. Jake passed an energy conglomerate, a telecoms giant. Then he saw it.

Granble Mining Company.

He took a deep breath and passed through the door. A guard put his arm out.

'Can I help you?'

Jake made a show of patting his pockets, but he knew what he was looking for. From the back of his jeans he pulled out the exclusive invitation that he'd taken – well, *borrowed* – from his mum's handbag: *Mr Granble requests the pleasure of your company* . . .

The guard cast a quick glance over it, then waved Jake through.

The room contained maybe twenty people. Jake recognised a well-known rapper, but mostly it seemed to be suits. He guessed they were the sponsors whose money Granble was planning to steal. Marissa the pit bull was drinking a glass of champagne. She saw Jake, swallowed slowly and walked to the other side of the room.

Through the bodies, Jake saw Granble. He was sipping from a long drink. Marissa whispered something in his ear and he looked up. Granble's eyes went wide for a split second and Jake walked over towards him. There was no way Granble could touch him in here. Not in front of all these people.

When he got close, Granble waved Marissa away.

'You're sure?' she asked.

Granble nodded. He held out a hand to Jake.

'What a . . . *surprise*.'

'Not a pleasant one, I hope,' said Jake.

Granble's smile was fixed, and he clenched his fat fingers around Jake's. Jake squeezed back. He was stronger.

'I didn't expect to see you here,' said Granble. 'I heard you'd run away with that girlfriend of yours.'

From below in the stadium, booming music began to play. 'Diamonds Are a Girl's Best Friend'.

Jake nodded towards the viewing glass.

'Abri didn't want to miss the show,' he said. 'Why don't you take a look?'

Granble released the grip on Jake's hand and walked over to the glass. A few other suits were watching the show too. The catwalk had been laid out from the player tunnel halfway across the pitch. A giant screen at one end of the ground showed a close-up.

Abri Kuertzen was strutting her stuff along the runway, looking every inch the international supermodel. Jake felt Granble tense beside him. His cheek was twitching.

The plan's working.

'You'll see she's wearing a particularly special piece of jewellery,' Jake said. 'One of Granble's finest. Thing is, we both know it could be out of a Christmas cracker.'

189

Granble seized Jake's arm, and pulled him away. Marissa noticed, but pointed out on to the pitch, focusing the attention of the other guests. 'We call that particular piece the Star of Mozambique. One hundred and twenty-five carats –'

'Just who do you think you are, kid?' hissed Granble. 'You're one boy against *me*? I could crush you and your family in an instant.'

'Better send someone better than Jaap next time.'

Granble's face went red. 'What have you done to him?' he snapped.

'Let's just say his bell-ringing days are over,' said Jake, trying not to smirk too much.

Granble relaxed and backed off. 'In a country that has had as many problems as mine, there are always more Jaaps.' Granble gestured towards a door leading off the box. 'Why don't we talk somewhere more private?'

Jake had to think fast. He wasn't scared, if it was just the two of them. *But what if Granble had something up his sleeve?*

'*Don't do it,*' said a voice in his ear. '*Stay in the open.*'

But Jake knew Granble wasn't going to talk in the open. 'Sure,' said Jake.

'*Damn it, Jake. Can you hear me? I said that's a negative.*'

Granble led the way through the door. The room was like a small office, with a computer, a phone and two chairs.

A branded San Siro notepad rested on the desk. Jake guessed it must be for VIP spectators who needed to work at short notice, or make a private call.

There was no one else in the room. Granble let Jake enter, then shut the door.

'What do you want?'

'It's time to talk,' said Jake.

He wondered if his father had heard him. Those were the code words. This was his chance to make the plan work. All he had to do was make him confess.

'Time is something you don't have,' said Granble.

Jake's throat felt a little tight. He could imagine what Granble must be like to do business with across a boardroom table. The tycoon was leaning back against the desk, looking as cool as the iced drink he was holding.

'I know you're trying to defraud your investors out of millions,' said Jake.

Granble shrugged. 'My investors are looking at handsome returns, thank you very much.'

'Not if word gets out that your mines are duds,' said Jake, 'and all your diamonds are fake.'

'Unsubstantiated,' said Granble. 'All you have is *one* phoney diamond necklace that you *claim* belongs to me. Boy, you don't get where I am without making enemies. Maybe one of my competitors is trying to bring me down.'

'Or a few supermodels,' said Jake. 'Doesn't say much for you, if you can be outwitted by three walking coat-hangers.'

Granble flinched.

'It looks like I had the last laugh there, though, doesn't it?' said Granble. 'From what I heard, Mademoiselles Sienna and Monique met their untimely ends today.'

It wasn't quite an admission of guilt. Jake could see that Granble was a cagey crim.

'But Abri escaped,' said Jake.

'Oh, so she did,' said Granble. 'But . . . South Africa . . .' Granble was clearly choosing his words carefully, '. . . is a . . . *dangerous* country . . . especially for a pretty young thing like her.'

Granble sneered, but Jake could see he was riled.

'You really think you'll get away with it, don't you?' Jake asked. His anger was real enough now.

'I know I will,' Granble coolly replied. 'The mines might be worthless, but this time next week I'll have disappeared. With all my money. And you know the funniest thing?'

'Go on,' said Jake. He was trying to keep the grin off his face.

'The funniest thing is going to be the knowledge that you're dead.'

Granble burst into laughter, long hard guffaws. He wiped his eyes, and gave a manic whoop.

Half a second later, the sound reverberated back through the ground's tannoy. Granble's head snapped round.

'What was that?' he said.

'That was you admitting you're a crook to eighty thousand spectators,' Jake said. He pulled the mic out of his pocket, and tapped it twice, then blew. The magnified sound blasted through the speakers.

Granble's face went white. He started to shake. He looked left and right, as though searching for a place to run. Jake opened the door, and gave a wide sweep of his arm.

'Your adoring fans await you,' Jake said.

Granble pushed past him and pelted through.

Outside, the smartly dressed sponsors all stood in silence, looking on. Marissa was nowhere to be seen.

'I can explain . . .' Granble began.

'The handsome returns?' Jake reminded them.

A few seconds later, four policemen burst into the VIP box. They broke through the angry crowd and one of them showed Granble his badge.

'Detective Ignacio Semprina. You're under arrest, Mr Granble, for murder and industrial fraud . . .'

As Granble was being read his rights, Jake went over to the

viewing panel. The ground was silent, and thousands of faces were turned up towards the box. On the runway stood Abri, looking up at him. The TV relay screen showed her twenty feet tall. She blew him a kiss.

Jake wished he could get down there to be with her, but chaos had erupted in the room behind him. Granble was protesting his innocence, while the police were holding back a sponsor who was grasping for Granble's throat and shouting something in what might have been Spanish.

The rapper came up to Jake, and was pulling the diamond rings off his fingers. He dropped them in a discarded champagne glass. 'That asshole owes me so much money.'

Jake turned back towards the stadium, to admire Abri again.

But she was gone.

The camera still lingered on where she had been. All that remained in the close-up frame was her necklace, sparkling in the spotlights.

23

Jake's mum released him from a ten-second hug that was close to crushing his ribcage.

'I don't want to say I'm proud of you,' she said, 'because what you did was stupid. Stupid and dangerous. But . . .' she squeezed him again, '. . . I *am* proud of you.'

Jake laughed, and gave his dad a sideways glance. His mum didn't know everything. She'd said she didn't *want* to know. His dad and he had come up with a story that prompted as many questions as it answered. It didn't include MI6. It missed out everything about rooftop combat, snipers and assassins in a neglected church. But if she didn't know the means, she knew the end.

The whole world did.

Granble was facing the rest of his natural life behind bars. The only question was where he'd serve his lengthy sentence. Several different governments wanted him extradited.

Jake's dad said that Marissa had been very helpful with their enquiries. So much for the loyal pit bull.

'More of a puppy,' his dad had joked.

So here they both stood, cases packed, by the check-in desks at Milan airport. It had been less than a week since Jake and his dad had arrived. He'd met Abri right here, albeit when she was dressed in a black balaclava and robbing his mother. There'd been no word of her since the half-time show, but something told Jake that she probably wouldn't be going back to modelling. Jake's dad had suggested that whoever did end up prosecuting Granble might need her testimony, but that would entail a witness protection programme and a change of identity. Jake couldn't imagine anyone that beautiful managing to hide for long. But he knew it was right that she disappear.

Their flight came up on the display as 'ready to board'.

'We gotta go,' said Jake. 'We still haven't checked in.'

'Hopefully you'll be better off in London than here,' said his mum. 'It was nice having you with me though, Jake.'

'You should come over soon,' said Jake. 'They have clothes there too, y'know.'

His mum laughed. 'Maybe I will. But you need to stay away from models for a while. Football's safer than fashion.'

Jake stifled his laughter, pretending it was a cough.

'Take care, Steve,' said his mum.

His parents attempted a hug, and ended up looking like awkward relatives.

Jake picked up his case and headed towards the check-in desk. His dad came after him. As they waited, his dad said, 'Your mum and I have been talking. About this Olympic Advantage thing . . .'

Jake had forgotten all about it in the aftermath of Granble's arrest.

'Listen, Dad,' he said. 'I understand. It's a long way –'

'We think you should go.'

Jake almost dropped his case. 'You're kidding!'

'Nope.'

'To Florida! For two weeks?'

'As long as you –'

'– stay out of trouble?' Jake finished for him.

'You're a quick learner.'

They went through passport control and duty free, where his dad bought a bottle of Jameson. At the gate, Jake's dad opened a paperback, and Jake found a copy of *Il Giorno*, the Italian daily newspaper.

While the front headlines were full of Granble's arrest, the sports pages told of England's remarkable second-half performance and Mark Fortune's first international hat-trick.

Jake could just about piece it together. England hadn't won the Brotherhood Tournament, but they were acknowledged as being the team to watch. All young players, ripe for the future. Maybe if the Florida camp went well, he'd get to join them.

One day.

'Mr Bastin?' said a voice.

Jake lowered his paper at the same time his dad looked up from his book. A man in a pristine white suit stood in front of them. Everything about him was crisp and clean, like he was sculpted from wax. His black hair was greased back, not a strand out of place. In his hand was a briefcase.

'Can I help you?' his dad asked politely.

'I apologise for the intrusion,' he said, with a flash of white teeth. 'I have a gift for you.' He had a slight accent that Jake couldn't place.

Jake bristled. This man emanated an aura of threat, of danger.

Jake's dad stood up.

'I'm afraid we don't know who you are,' he said. 'Please leave us alone.'

The man took a step back. 'Of course, of course. You don't know me, but you know my employer.' He laid out the briefcase on the table, and flicked open the catches.

Jake was on red alert, ready to pounce if this slimeball tried anything.

But all the man pulled out was a folded copy of *The Times* and two ornate leather boxes. He turned them round and opened them. Inside were two identical watches.

'From Russia, with love,' he said, closed the case and walked swiftly away. He paced effortlessly between a crowd of travellers walking in the opposite direction.

Jake picked up one of the boxes and looked closely at the face. It was a Rolex, encrusted with diamonds and a silvery metal that Jake guessed was platinum. He knew enough about watches to realise this one would have cost upwards of ten thousand pounds. A small tag was attached. In tiny script was written: 'With gratitude. I. P.'

'Igor Popov . . .' Jake said.

His dad had picked up the paper and was reading an article at the bottom of the page. The headline was 'Russia reaps the benefit of South African diamond fraud'.

Jake only had to read a few lines to understand the gist of the piece: Granble's deception had triggered a huge fall in stock-market confidence, which was affecting even the legitimate South African diamond houses. Mines owned by wealthy Russians like Popov were picking up the slack in the supply chain.

'So Popov wins again,' said Jake.

'His time will come,' his dad said coolly.

Jake felt like throwing the watch on the floor and crushing it to tiny pieces with his heel. Instead he took a few deep breaths and fastened it on to his wrist. It was heavier than he thought it would be.

His dad looked at him with a confused frown.

Jake made sure he didn't blink. 'Just so I don't forget.'

COMING IN FEBRUARY 2011

STRIKER
THE
EDGE

Jake can't believe he's been scouted for Olympic Advantage. It's a dream come true to train with the top teenage athletes from around the world . . . these are the kids that will go on to win gold medals. His dad has come along but promises to stay behind the scenes; this is Jake's moment.

But the sunny Florida camp is hiding a nasty secret. The German weight-lifter is crushed by a barbell, painkillers are being issued illegally and many of the athletes are getting seriously aggressive. Jake knows something is up, and he's in the perfect position to report back to MI6.

It's his first mission on his own. Popov will be watching . . .

EGMONT PRESS: ETHICAL PUBLISHING

Egmont Press is about turning writers into successful authors and children into passionate readers – producing books that enrich and entertain. As a responsible children's publisher, we go even further, considering the world in which our consumers are growing up.

Safety First
Naturally, all of our books meet legal safety requirements. But we go further than this; every book with play value is tested to the highest standards – if it fails, it's back to the drawing-board.

Made Fairly
We are working to ensure that the workers involved in our supply chain – the people that make our books – are treated with fairness and respect.

Responsible Forestry
We are committed to ensuring all our papers come from environmentally and socially responsible forest sources.

For more information, please visit our website at www.egmont.co.uk/ethical